ANGEL'S

PR

An enthral[illegible] mystery full of twists

ROGER SILVERWOOD

Yorkshire Murder Mysteries Book 28

JOFFE BOOKS

Joffe Books, London
www.joffebooks.com

First published in Great Britain in 2021

ISBN: 978-1-80405-008-8

‘When you’re going to be murdered,
it doesn’t matter what you know.’

ONE

Meeting Room Two, Feathers Hotel, Bromersley, South Yorkshire
Thursday, 18 March, 3 p.m.

On the meeting-room door was a sign neatly handwritten on a piece of card. It read, *The Tiddlywinks Association. Private. Members only.*

Inside the room, all the attendees were already seated. A big man sat at the head of the table. He was Alexander Velleman, the host of the meeting.

Velleman said, 'My sources have located a case of twenty-two assorted guns that have been confiscated by the police.'

The man to his right, James Robertson, said, 'Fantastic! Can we get at them?'

The other six men at the table in lounge suits, collars and ties nodded their enthusiastic support.

'Indeed, James. It will enable me to expand my operations beyond two counties,' Velleman said, blowing a cloud of blue cigar smoke into the little meeting room. 'At first the north of the country, then the Midlands . . . who knows? In time, the entire country.'

Robertson said, 'We could get rid of Angel, for one thing.'

Velleman's face changed. 'No, I don't want him shot,' he said. 'His pain would be over in a second. I have a much more sophisticated way to get rid of him *and* keep him out of my hair for ever. Leave him to me.'

'What's the plan?' said Oscar Starr, the accountant and general manager of the group.

Velleman turned to Robertson. 'It's an operation for one fit man with a gun. Are you fit? Are you still going to the gym?'

'I do a full workout every day,' Robertson said.

'Good. Keep that up and the job's yours.'

'I won't let you down.'

'You'd better not. You'll need a black pickup truck. If it's not black, it wants spraying. Change the plates, of course.'

'I'll see to that,' said a man from the bottom of the table.

'Right. We shall want it by Tuesday.'

'No problem.'

'Top security. No comebacks if the police should get hold of the truck.'

'No problem, Alex.'

'On all matters of security talk to me. On necessary expenditure, liaise with Oscar. Now, all of you, shut your mouths and listen. This is what we have to do . . .'

* * *

RAOC depot, Invercockileeky, Scotland
Thursday, 25 March, 2 a.m.

In the dead of night, a black pickup truck drove up to the electrified fence of the huge RAOC depot in Invercockileeky, in the wilds sixty miles north-east of Glasgow.

A man in a dark suit, black shirt, black trainers and a balaclava jumped out of the pickup and took a short roll of electric cable and a pair of long-handled wire cutters out of the truck. Wearing heavy-duty rubber gloves, he connected one end of the electric cable to the security fence, then unrolled it across the grass and connected the other end to the fence, three metres away — rewiring the circuit in a matter of minutes. Then he began to snip away at the fence, cutting a big enough gap for him to be able to drive the pickup through it.

It was government land that had been a military airport in the Second World War, later having been converted to an RAOC storage and distribution depot. There were thirty or more buildings, some converted aeroplane hangars, others brick-built warehouses and offices. It stored the requirements of the British army: everything from pins to armoured tanks. In addition, the RAOC stored and distributed miscellaneous items for civil defence and for the police, from road diversion signs to light armaments.

The camp was in darkness except for the two windows of the night duty office and communications room. These were on the second floor of the purpose-built block of offices and accommodation for officers and men stationed there.

The man in the balaclava drove the pickup into the camp, looking for Hangar 16. All the buildings were clearly marked with large numbers in black and white, but each one was up to half a mile away from the next. However, it didn't take long to find it. He parked the pickup on the side out of sight of the night duty office. Then he took out a jemmy and a coil of rope, which he pulled over his head and put an arm through so that it hung on him in a diagonal fashion.

He opened the door with the jemmy and went inside. The size of the hangar was immense. He shone his torch at the aisles. There were at least twenty, with shelving on each side and some shelves reaching up to twenty metres high.

He pointed the torch around the walls and found a huge guide pasted on the wall. It listed headings, in alphabetic order, of the categories of items in that particular hangar.

The category he wanted was stored at the top of one of the highest shelves. He shoved the torch in his pocket and put the jemmy on a lower shelf. Using the shelves as steps and the verticals to hold on to, he scaled the shelving easily enough. Scrambling around on the very top shelf, with the roof less than ten centimetres above his head, he found what he wanted. He shone his torch on the stencilled black printing on the small sealed wooden crate. It read: *9223564588210 ASSTD SIDEARMS 22*. He sighed with relief.

He tried to move it, but it wouldn't budge. He put down the torch and using both hands managed to lift it, but it was too heavy for him to carry on his shoulder down to the bottom.

He lifted the rope over his head and uncoiled it. Then he fastened the end around the centre of the crate and gently lowered it to the concrete floor.

Suddenly he heard footsteps.

He turned off the torch.

He sucked in air and held his breath.

In the distance, he saw a uniformed man come through the big double doors at the far end of the hangar, carrying a torch. The beam seemed as powerful as a searchlight looking for aircraft in the sky, and his footsteps on the concrete floor resounded throughout the hangar.

In the dim light, the man in black looked down at the crate he had just lowered, and the rope still hanging down attached to it. His muscles tightened. The uniformed man couldn't miss them, and he seemed to be walking very quickly now down the far aisle, waving the torch here and there. He hadn't much time.

The man in black quickly and silently climbed down the shelves to the hangar floor. He picked up the heavy crate and pushed it into a space on the nearest shelf. Then he coiled up the rope and shoved it as far as he could between the shelves.

The guard was checking each aisle systematically. Up one aisle, turning at the end of it, going down the next and so on. He was only two aisles away.

The man in black glanced round for somewhere to hide. He looked around the lower shelves and found a space between some small boxes to climb into. He grabbed the jemmy and squeezed between the shelves and equipment.

As he shuffled into position, he could hear the loud and positive footsteps of the guard getting nearer and nearer. Eventually he reached the aisle where both the crate and the man in black were hidden. He was walking quickly and flashing the light here and there as he pressed along.

He was quite close when the footsteps suddenly stopped.

The man in black sucked in a short breath and held it. His grip on the jemmy tightened. His heart was beating so hard he could hear the pulsing in his ears.

The guard pointed his torch along the shelf where the man in black was hiding. Then he grabbed one of his feet, tugged it, and in a broad Scottish accent said, 'Get yoursel' oot o' there and be quick aboot it.'

The Scotsman shone his torch into of the eyes of the man in black and snatched the jemmy from his hand as he struggled to squeeze out from between the shelves.

'You'll not be needing this, laddie,' he said, and with tremendous energy threw the jemmy halfway down the aisle.

'Hurry along there,' he said.

The man in black stood up and peered at his assailant. The Scot was big and broad with a face like suntanned granite. He held aloft a big black truncheon.

'Take that balaclava off,' he snapped. 'Let's be looking at you.'

The man took a step towards the Scot, raised both his hands, and pulled off the balaclava, holding it at his waist.

The Scotsman stared at his captive's face while, under cover of the balaclava, the man in black pulled a Walther from his waistband, pointed it at the Scotsman and pulled the trigger.

The Scotsman grabbed his chest, dropped to his knees, then fell down face forward and hit the concrete floor, dead.

The man in black put the balaclava back on. He picked up the wooden case of handguns, loaded it into the pickup truck, and drove away like a greyhound chasing a rabbit.

* * *

Order Room 1, Bromersley Police Station, South Yorkshire
Monday, 29 March, 11 a.m.

All officers of the rank of sergeant and above, eighteen in total, had been summoned at very short notice to the order room.

There were three chairs at the front, behind a trestle table with a jug of water and three glasses on it. Detective Superintendent Horace Harker had finished checking, by a roll call, that all were present, and had subsequently rushed out of the room with his clipboard.

The personnel were seated in front of the table in two rows, forming a rough semi-circle, and in no particular order. Detective Inspector Michael Angel with his team of two sergeants were in the second row.

Angel leaned forward to his opposite number in the uniformed branch, Inspector Asquith, who was sitting immediately in front of him. 'What's this all about, Haydn?' he whispered.

Asquith shook his head. 'No idea. Unless you've been stuffing old copies of *Health and Beauty* down the bog again.'

There were controlled titters in that quarter of the room.

At that moment Harker, Chief Constable Leon MacAndrews and a smartly uniformed woman came into the room.

Everybody stopped talking and stood up.

MacAndrews said, 'Thank you everybody, please sit down.'

The chief remained standing. When they were settled he began.

'I have asked you all here at very short notice to hear and welcome Commander Ann Deloitte, who has an urgent and important message for us.' He held out an open hand in her direction. 'Commander Deloitte.'

'Good morning,' she began. 'Time is precious. I will be brief.'

Angel thought that although physically she was every bit a woman — she had a pretty mouth, well-groomed hair and slim legs — she walked, stood and talked like a man. She stood erect, sticking out her chest and squeezing in her bottom.

'I want to cover as many stations as I can, as quickly as I can,' she said. 'It has come to the attention of Special Branch that . . . erm . . . certain law-breakers, shall we call them, are marshalling gangs of specialised criminals. The gangs are sometimes twelve-strong and are being formed in several ways. The strongest gangs are headed by one or two criminals, who enrol skilled but weaker personnel by finding out a weak spot in each of their prospective members so as to be able to get a hold over them. This applies throughout that gang and at all levels, which means the fear of the action of the leaders is frequently more than the fear of being caught by the law.

'Another phenomenon is that the gangs are run on military lines. They train and appoint specialists in certain aspects of lawbreaking. For instance, you will have heard recently of the little man in Newcastle who was found to own property in Newcastle, Leeds, York and Gateshead worth many millions of pounds. When he was interviewed by the National Crime Agency, he was unwilling to tell them how he came by the funds to purchase them. He was, of course, doing a very bad job of laundering the illicit cash receipts of the Enderby brothers' gang, which you will also have heard of.

'The Enderby brothers even had a man responsible for setting up alibis for characters in the front line. That's all he did all day, every day . . . made sure that everybody who did anything dishonest would have a well-planned alibi to cover him. In the same way, they had two men on security duty checking that property to be occupied by the gang was free of bugs and listening devices. They even have places to train as well as hide themselves or whoever they might have kidnapped . . . isolated places, farmhouses, places like that.

'All this sounds . . . discouraging, impossible to overcome . . . but it isn't. As well as all the excellent training and support you have here in Bromersley, across the country there are forty-two other matchless chief constables ready to pounce on the first sign of any gangland activity on their patches. They are well armed to deal with it — as, of course, are you.

'The reason for my visit today is to apprise you of the development of new crime methods so that you are prepared for more subtle approaches to criminal acts. Even if you are investigating some trivial offence that suggests any of the new techniques are being used, you must report it to your immediate superior. And if it is found to be valid, please report it to me at Special Branch, so that we can put together a national picture and eliminate the new practice.'

* * *

3 Ceresforth Drive, Bromersley, South Yorkshire
Monday, 5 April, 10 a.m.

A vintage Rolls-Royce, driven by a liveried chauffeur, turned through the wrought-iron gates, went round the private drive to the front of the mansion and stopped. A big man got out of the back of the car, took a black leather bag off the seat and closed the door.

The Rolls whispered away.

The man then went up the stone steps to the arched double doors and pressed the doorbell, before letting himself in and going straight to the drawing room.

A small old lady in a wheelchair turned to him and with a big smile said, 'Good morning, Doctor.'

'Now, Mrs Figgis, how are we today?' the big man said as he put his bag down at the side of her wheelchair.

The old lady looked a little disappointed. 'I thought you were going to call me Charlotte, William dear?'

'Of course, my dear Charlotte,' he said, and kissed her lightly on the cheek. 'And how are you today?'

She patted the chair nearest to her. 'Sit down. It's this pain, William. The same as yesterday. Right down my back and down both legs. It isn't any easier. If you could get rid of that I could . . . maybe . . . go on a few more years.'

Dr Hart looked across at her. 'I have just the very thing, my dear Charlotte. A new drug that numbs all that pain in your bones and brings absolute peace. You'll never complain again.'

The old lady's eyes brightened. 'That would be absolutely marvellous, William.'

'And there are no side effects. You simply sleep like a baby. You need have no worry. By the way, where is your home help today?'

Mrs Figgis smiled. 'Don't you remember? On a Thursday she comes at one o'clock. You asked me yesterday.'

'Of course I did, dear Charlotte. So, there's only you and me in this big house then?'

Mrs Figgis smiled. 'Yes. That's right. It's very . . . erm, cosy, isn't it?'

Dr Hart nodded.

Mrs Figgis fluttered her colourless eyelashes at him. 'By the way, William, I have something for you. Something you need to continue with your philanthropic work.'

'Oh,' he said. 'And what's that, my dear Charlotte?'

She reached down to her capacious handbag, took out a long brown envelope and passed it to him with a big smile.

The doctor took it eagerly. He looked at it and noticed that it had his name printed on the front. Then he looked at Mrs Figgis.

'Oh, Charlotte,' he said. He stood up leaned over towards her and gave her another light kiss on the cheek. 'May I open it? May I read it?'

'Of course. That should go a good way towards paying for that orphanage you want to open if anything happens to me.'

'Oh, Charlotte, thank you,' he said, briefly looking up from reading it. 'That's really wonderful, what you're doing for your community. And I shall call it "The Charlotte Figgis Home for Orphans"!'

The old lady beamed.

The doctor folded up the papers, returned them to the envelope and put it into his inside jacket pocket. Then he pulled his bag closer to his feet, opened it and began fishing around in the bottom of it.

'What are you doing, William?'

'I am preparing to give you an injection of that gentle painkilling drug, Charlotte . . . that new drug that will free you from pain in your back and legs for ever.'

'Oh, yes,' Mrs Figgis said. 'Are you going to give it to me in my arm?'

'Yes, Charlotte dear,' he said as he stuck the needle into the ampoule and began to draw the drug down into the syringe.

She watched him and began to roll up her sleeve.

Then in a very loud but shaky voice, she said, '*Inspector Angel. Come in now, quickly, please!*'

Immediately the double doors to the hall opened and Detective Inspector Angel burst in, followed by two male PCs and a female detective sergeant.

Dr Hart's face went white. 'What's this?' he said. 'Who are you? What are doing? What's happening?'

Angel snatched the syringe from the doctor. 'Read him his rights, Sergeant.'

The two PCs grabbed the man's arms, handcuffed them behind his back and marched him out of the room, followed by DS Flora Carter, who began, 'William Hart, I am arresting you on suspicion of murder and attempted murder. You do not have to say anything . . .'

The door closed.

Angel put the loaded syringe in the doctor's bag. 'Now, how are you, Mrs Figgis? That was a marvellous piece of acting. You could put Judi Dench out of business!'

The old lady sighed. 'I may have sounded all right, but I was terrified, to tell the truth, Inspector. I was shaking all over.'

'You got it off down pat, Mrs Figgis,' Angel said. 'We have it all on tape. And by the look of it, there's enough diamorphine hydrochloride in this syringe to kill an elephant.'

'I only did it for the sake of my dear friend Beatrice.'

'Don't you worry, Mrs Figgis. Now he'll be tried for the murder of Beatrice Philpot *and* Clarice Seaman. *And* for what he tried to do to you here today.'

TWO

Jeeves the Jewellers, 22–24 Market Street, Bromersley, South Yorkshire
Tuesday, 6 April, 9 a.m.

Sydney Fluke walked into the shop and looked around. His jaw was working overtime. It was always so. He had the habit of chewing gum, which his mother said was to hide the smell of lager on his breath.

Jeeves the Jewellers was brightly lit and there were four large glass counters, each one manned by an assistant — three young men and a young woman. At that moment, Sydney Fluke was the only customer in the shop.

All the assistants quietly listened and watched every move Fluke made. It relieved the boredom.

The assistant polishing the nearest glass counter quickly disposed of the duster and smiled at Fluke. 'Can I help you?'

'Yes. I am looking for a really nice engagement ring for . . . a lass.'

'Yes, sir. Well, we have a very wide selection of rings. Did you have a particular stone in mind?'

'Oh, diamond,' Fluke said firmly. 'Definitely diamond.'

The assistant pointed down into the showcase at a particular pad of fifteen rings, mostly with beautiful, glittering ice-clear diamonds.

'Do you see anything there you like?'

Sydney Fluke bent forward. His eyes glowed. 'Yes, hmm . . . there might be something.'

The assistant unlocked the sliding glass door, reached in for the pad and put it on the counter. 'There. Some of those rings are solitaire diamonds set in platinum, and the diamonds are over a carat.'

The young man's eyes were all over the pad. He stopped chewing as his eyes settled on the ring with the largest stone. Then with a skinny, sweaty finger he pointed at it.

'Can I see *that* one?' he said.

'Certainly, sir,' the assistant said and he took it out of its slot looked at the ticket. 'That's a 2.25-carat solitaire diamond. And it is priced at £3,800.'

Fluke took the ring. His eyes sparkled. With his tongue he moved the gum to the other side of his mouth and stopped chewing.

He examined the ring from all angles . . . as subtly as if he was considering buying a house brick.

The assistant said, 'If you care to bring the young lady in, we will size it to fit her finger. There is no charge for that.'

After a few moments, Fluke's eyes wandered back to the pad of the fourteen other rings standing on top of the counter. He picked up the pad.

The assistant's stomach churned. He licked his lips and moved a step closer to Fluke. 'Erm . . . can I help you, sir?'

'No. No. It's all right,' he said.

Fluke tried one or two other rings on, looked at the prices on the labels and finally put the rings back on the pad. He put it back on the counter. 'I'll have to go to the post office. I'll be back. Thank you.'

He made for the door.

The assistant glanced at the tray, saw that all the fifteen ring slots were filled and sighed with relief. 'Thank you, sir. Look forward to seeing you.'

Fluke nodded and went out.

No sooner had the door closed when Mr Jeeves, the proprietor, appeared from nowhere.

He rapidly approached the assistant who had been showing rings to Fluke. 'Marshall, I don't like that sort of character. They never buy anything but they take every opportunity to steal. Have you checked that tray of rings?'

'Yes, Mr Jeeves. It's full.'

'Let me see.' Jeeves took the pad and went through each ring.

Then he suddenly bellowed. 'Here! Look at this.' He held something up between finger and thumb. 'A highly polished ring pull from a lager can!'

He turned to the other assistants. 'Right, everybody get after him. He can't have got far!'

The three assistants left their counters and rushed out of the shop into the street.

Then Jeeves turned to Marshall. 'Ring 999 and inform the police. Hurry up!'

* * *

Interview Room 1, Bromersley Police Station, South Yorkshire
Tuesday, 6 April, 10 a.m.

PC Weightman brought Sydney Fluke into the interview room. He confidently chewed his gum and managed an arrogant grin at DI Angel and DS Flora Carter as they followed him in.

Angel looked up at the tall burly PC. 'Thank you, Constable, you can stand down and return to your regular duties.'

'Right, sir,' Weightman said and left the room.

Fluke was already seated at the small table in the centre of the room. He clearly knew the drill.

Even so, the man's rights needed restating. Angel said, 'This is interview will be recorded, and I'm sure you're no stranger to how this goes. You do not have to say anything. But it may harm your defence if you do not mention when questioned something which you later rely on in court.' He paused, finger hovering over the button on the recorder. 'It's like this, Mr Fluke. The proprietor of that store you stole from wants one thing . . . and that's his ring returned. Give it back and this ends now. Mr Jeeves is prepared to drop all charges against you.'

Fluke sniffed. 'I haven't got his effing ring. And I think all you coppers and Jeeves and his boys are taking a dead liberty assuming I'd steal anything. I'm not a thief.'

'Save it for the tape, Mr Fluke.'

Angel pressed *record*.

'It is 10.50 a.m. on 6 April. Interview of Sydney Fluke, twenty-six, unemployed . . . present, DI Michael Angel and DS Flora Carter. Tell me what happened to you earlier this morning, Mr Marshall.'

'I haven't got his effing ring. I'm willing to be searched. Save all this time-wasting rubbish. Will that satisfy Mr Jeeves?'

Angel sighed. 'I think you already know the answer to that.'

* * *

DI Angel's office, Bromersley Police Station, South Yorkshire
Thursday, 8 April, 10 a.m.

Angel was going through the post and his eye caught the front page of the *Police Review*.

EX-POLICE CHIEF MURDERED

Retired police officer Chief Inspector Angus Wilde, sixty-two, was on security duty at the RAOC depot at Invercockileeky when he was shot dead by robbers, who escaped with a cache of lethal hand guns. (Full story on page 8.)

Angel ruminated on what he had just read. Another dead policeman. He was sorry for the man who had been murdered and his family, but he was also thinking that the theft of those handguns could be to tool up a gang. That was the new pattern of life in the UK. But wherever the weapons were destined to go, those guns on the streets in the wrong hands could kill hundreds of people . . . yes, and it could take years before every one of them would be taken out of the hands of crooks and evil people.

His ruminations were disturbed by noises in the corridor outside his office. He could hear raised voices and scuffling sounds. He threw down the magazine and opened the door.

PC Weightman was dragging a reluctant Sydney Fluke down the corridor.

'What's going on, Constable?' Angel said.

'This young fellow doesn't want to go in a cell, sir,' Weightman said.

'What's he been charged with?'

Before Weightman could reply, Fluke said, 'I only knocked this bloke's helmet off. I shouldn't go to prison for that. I want to make a statement.'

'He won't pay the fine, sir,' Weightman said.

Angel nodded and turned to Fluke. 'Sydney, *why* did you knock the constable's helmet off?'

Fluke shrugged. 'I dunno.' He grinned. 'Seemed like a good idea at the time.'

Angel frowned and shook his head.

'I want to make a statement,' Fluke repeated.

Angel frowned. 'What about?'

Fluke looked thoughtfully down at his hands. Firstly, he examined his palms, then he turned his hands over and looked at his dirty, ill-kept fingernails . . .

'Well?' Angel said.

Fluke looked up. 'Well, I can't make a statement out here!'

'All right, come in my office.' Angel looked up at Weightman. 'We can talk to Sydney in my office. Come on, Constable.'

Fluke's eyes flashed and he started struggling again. 'No! I don't want to go in there!'

'Why not?' Angel said.

'I just don't.'

Angel looked at the young man thoughtfully. 'All right, put him in a cell.'

'No!' Fluke said. 'OK, I'll go in the office.'

When all three men were seated and the door was closed, Angel said, 'Right, Sydney, I'm all ears.'

Fluke frowned and looked down at his hands again and began to bite his lip.

'Is it about that diamond ring, Sydney? Did you want to say that you *had* taken it after all?'

'No. No!' Fluke shouted. 'It wasn't that. I *never* took the ring. It was something else, but I've forgotten.'

Angel sighed. His face tightened and he looked at Weightman. 'He's just wasting our time, Constable. Lock him up.'

* * *

Angel spent the rest of that day ploughing through junior officers' reports from the last month and getting his own reports done. He reached the end of a week, so he stopped and looked at his watch: 5.36. He threw down his pen and closed his computer.

And so he came to the end of another weary day. There seemed to be more crime about than ever before. He reached out for his hat and left the office.

Angel lived three miles away from the station in a modern bungalow on the Forest Hill Estate. It took him only a few minutes in the BMW.

As he approached his home, 30 Park Street, he could see a big black car parked in front of the bungalow. He didn't recognise it and frowned. As he got nearer he could see that it was parked right across the front of his garage doors.

He frowned again. There were no other cars on the entire length of the rest of the street. Why would anyone park in front of his garage doors? It was ridiculous. As he drove up to it, he bared his teeth.

He looked to see who was in the car. It was a large, imposing vehicle with lots of chrome shining in the low evening sun. A vintage Rolls-Royce, he thought. From his seat he couldn't see any signs of life.

He pulled on the break, switched off the ignition, opened his car door and leaped forth, determined to bawl the driver out.

As he walked towards the car he could see a man in the driving seat. He had a face like a ferret.

At the same time, two doors, one on each side of the big car, opened. Two men got out and advanced determinedly on Angel.

They were both big men with remarkably ugly faces, but were well-dressed, collar-and-tie types. One was fair-haired, almost white-blond; the other's hair was dark brown.

'Don't you know you're parked in front of my garage doors?' Angel stormed. 'You've the whole street to park in.'

'Keep your shirt on, Michael,' the fair-haired man said. 'We apologise. The boss wants to speak to you urgent, like.'

Angel's anger was immediately blunted by the man's attitude. Common sense had taken its place, and a shiver of excitement vibrated through his body. From their outward appearance, Angel knew he was in the hands of powerful criminals: organised crime, big time. He tried not to let it show.

'Well, he knows where he can reach me,' Angel said. 'I'm at the office from eight thirty to five o'clock, five days a week. He can also phone me anytime.'

The fair-haired one tensed. 'That's not how the boss works, Michael,' he said. 'He wants us to take you to him and bring you back. By the way, my name's Hans.'

Then the dark haired one said, 'It won't take long and it don't hurt one bit. And my name's Sebastian.'

Angel noticed that Sebastian had had his nose broken, and it had been reset somewhat badly. It caused him to talk nasally and repeatedly sniff.

They both walked close up to him, too close for comfort.

Angel took in the situation. One of the monsters he could perhaps deal with, but two would be more difficult.

'Now, if you would please move your car up the street, I can get my car in the garage,' Angel said.

As he spoke, the two men took up positions one each side of him, facing each other.

'If you don't mind, Michael, you can do that when you come back,' Hans said.

The two men edged even closer to Angel.

'No, thank you,' Angel said. Then he leaned forward slightly and jabbed each of the men hard in their stomachs with his elbows. They gasped and their heads came down in response to the pain and Angel caught each of them under their jaws in a most exacting double uppercut.

The blow caused Hans to fall heavily on his back. He looked dazed. He sat up, shook his head and put his hand to his jaw.

Sebastian came back straightaway. He locked one muscled arm round Angel's neck and squeezed hard while at the same time punching him in the face with his other hand. Angel bent down and managed to pull Sebastian over his back up in the air and down onto the pavement. With his arm still round Angel's neck, Sebastian pulled the policeman down onto the pavement with him.

Hans, now standing, bent down and grabbed one of Angel's arms and gripped it tightly.

'Get his other arm, Seb,' he said.

Sebastian grabbed Angel's other arm and the three men got to their feet. Then Hans pinioned both the inspector's arms behind his back, his hands facing outwards so that he couldn't bend his arms at the elbows.

Sebastian, now in front of Angel, looked into his face. 'Now, Mr Angel, you *are* coming with us. Have you got the message yet?'

Then he punched Angel hard in the stomach. It hurt.

Angel gasped and pulled against Hans's grip on his arms, but the blond man was too powerful.

Sebastian came at him again, but Angel lifted both his feet, kicked him in the chest and sent him reeling backwards onto the hard pavement. There was the sound of a sharp crack as his head hit the deck. His eyes scrunched up in obvious pain.

At the same moment, Hans had lost his balance and began staggering backwards, still holding onto Angel's arms. They fell together onto the pavement.

Hans lost his grip on Angel's right arm, so the policeman began a barrage of blows with his free fist at Hans's face. The fair-haired brute had to release his grip to defend himself.

Angel then sprang to his feet, whereas Hans reached his feet much more slowly, and Angel punched him several times on the jaw while he was straightening himself up. The blows landed well, but it didn't seem to affect the big man much. Hans reciprocated but Angel pulled back, avoiding most of the impact. Then Angel mounted a powerful right blow to his jaw, followed by a sharp left.

Hans advanced on Angel, throwing out blow after blow. Angel managed to dodge most of them.

Hans backed Angel up against the Rolls-Royce then held him against it by the throat and aimed a powerful blow to his face. Angel managed to divert the direction of the blow, and Hans's fist hit the upright between the windows of the big car with a mighty blow. He yelled out with pain and held his wrist to his chest.

The ferrety little driver in livery and peaked hat looked on from his seat in the car with eyebrows raised, as if fighting was beneath him.

Angel grabbed Hans's collar with his left hand and delivered a mighty trio of blows to his chin that sent Hans down to the pavement, where he hit his head again.

Angel, breathing heavily, straightened up, ran a hand through his hair, pulled up his tie and brushed his trousers and jacket down. He looked across at the two monsters, who were holding their heads and shaking them.

Then suddenly, Angel felt a Boeing 747 hit his head from behind. He saw rockets and Catherine wheels and then all went black.

* * *

'I think he's coming round . . . Yeah. He is. There you are, Michael. Come on . . . Do you want a drink of water? . . . Are you all right?'

Angel blinked at the sound of the strange voice, then realised he had the king of all headaches. He opened his eyes. He was on a bed with another ugly man leaning over him, this time a smaller fellow. He looked in his sixties, had a greying moustache and wore an expensive dark suit.

Angel took a wary sip of the water, then gulped the lot. He handed back the empty glass. 'Who are you?'

The little man smiled. 'Nobody.'

Angel frowned. 'Where am I?'

'You're at the Feathers Hotel.'

Angel looked around. Hans was standing with his back to the door and Sebastian was leaning against a wardrobe, one eye on the racing page of a newspaper and the other on Angel himself.

Angel could also see through the window. In the distance was a building he thought he recognised. It was an old stone-built mill from the 1800s. He was relieved he was still in Bromersley.

Hans said, 'Shall I tell Mr Velleman that he's awake?'

'*Don't use names,* you bloody fool,' the little man said explosively. 'It's just Alex. Remember, *just Alex.*'

'*He* won't have noticed,' Hans said. 'He's still half out of his mind. Look at him.'

'I could have you out on your frigging ear for that. I've only got to tell Alex and he'd have you cut down.'

Hans swallowed and with a trembling lip said, 'He wouldn't let *me* go.'

'Huh. Don't fool yourself.'

Hans lowered his voice almost to a whisper. 'You wouldn't tell him, would you? It just slipped out.'

'If you want to continue breathing, just watch your tongue,' the little man said softly, then he made for the door. He stopped and said in a louder voice, 'Get Angel ready. Wake him up. Make him presentable. Don't waste any time.'

The little man went out.

* * *

Ten minutes later, Angel found himself in a small sitting room, along with one other man opposite. The lump at the back of his head still throbbed, but he was determined it wouldn't affect whatever was ahead of him. He looked his sharp-dressed companion up and down. He reckoned that the man was in a Reid and Taylor suit that must have cost over six hundred pounds, and an equally smart shirt and tie. Good tailoring seemed mandatory for membership in this dangerous gang of thugs.

'Well, let's get down to it, Mr Angel,' Velleman said. 'My name is Alex and I want to speak to you about a man you've arrested by the name of William Hart.'

Angel stayed quiet.

'Now, I know Dr Hart personally,' Velleman continued, 'and I have found him to be a brilliant doctor. I understand that he is charged with the murder of two old ladies and attempting to murder a third. Now, Michael, he may have *marginally* over-prescribed a drug universally accepted as an analgesic, which tragically resulted in the death of two old ladies — who were, I understand, in severe pain and tired of life anyway. But otherwise in his brilliant career he has saved many, *many* lives. It seems that given the way the evidence will be presented, Hart will lose the case and be imprisoned. And clearly, this would not be justice.

'We realise that you can reverse this outcome easily by, say, losing a witness and adjusting some of the statements . . . or you could allow the doctor to escape by some means. In this way, the good doctor would be able to continue his life-saving work somewhere in the world . . . perhaps one of those African countries where doctors are so desperately needed.

'I realise that this may require a certain amount of rule-breaking on your part . . . it will perhaps result in a little embarrassment . . . so I am prepared to compensate you for that by making a one-off, tax-free, cash payment of twenty thousand pounds.'

Angel looked at the man but didn't reply.

'Yes, Michael. I said *twenty thousand pounds*. What do you say to that?'

Angel was thinking. Twenty thousand pounds would pay off his overdraft and his credit cards, knock a chunk off the mortgage and enable him to retire a few years earlier. All that would be fabulous, wonderful . . . however, he also knew that he would never be able to look at himself in a mirror again.

Angel slowly shook his head.

Velleman's eyebrows shot up. 'Not enough?' he said. 'What sort of a figure had you in mind then?'

'No thank you.'

The man in the six-hundred-pound suit rubbed his chin. 'Well, I suppose I could go up to twenty-*five* thousand pounds. But that would be tops. What do you say to that?'

Angel knew he was on dangerous ground. He could consider himself lucky if he got out of the building alive.

'There isn't enough money in the world that would persuade me to let a guilty man go free,' he said. 'And it doesn't matter how *you* interpret the case against William Hart, he's a murderer, a thief and a con man, and he needs to be locked away from ordinary, honest people.'

Velleman's face and cruel mouth tightened. Beads of perspiration appeared across his forehead.

'All very honourable, I'm sure,' he said with a hint of sarcasm. 'But I've already explained that the death of the woman was accidental.'

'And I've been advised by a surgeon that the amount of diamorphine hydrochloride in the syringe I took out of William Hart's hand would without doubt have killed his most recent victim. Each of the two other frail old ladies were injected with a similar amount by him and died soon afterwards.'

Velleman's face fell. He looked down at his tie. He pulled the lobe of his ear, then ran his fingers down his cheek to his bottom lip, which he squeezed several times.

Eventually he reached in his pocket for his expensive flip-screen mobile, tapped several keys, waited, then closed it. Seconds later, the door opened and Oscar put his head through. 'You wanted me, Alex?'

'Send the boys in,' he said.

'Right away,' Oscar said, and closed the door.

Angel quietly sighed. He wondered what was going to happen to him next.

Velleman turned back to him. 'I'm sorry that you choose not to be cooperative, Michael. You'll regret it, I assure you. My boys will return you to wherever they picked you up. This meeting never took place. Goodbye.'

* * *

It was six thirty when Angel arrived home. His chin was red raw, his suit was covered in patches of light-grey dust. One shoe was scuffed, his hair mussed, his tie tangled like rope and his collar askew. Despite his best attempts to tidy himself up after he had driven the car into the garage, it was impossible to hide the fact that he had been in a rumble.

As he slunk in through the back door, a voice from the kitchen said, 'That you, Michael? Seen the time?'

'Yes, sweetheart,' he called, hoping to reach the bedroom door to change his clothes before Mary saw him.

He was too late.

She reached the bedroom door. He turned away and began shrugging off his jacket.

'Don't you kiss me anymore when you come in?' she said.

'Of course.' He turned and stepped towards her.

She gasped at the sight of him.

'Just a minute.' Her tone sharpened. 'Have you seen what you've done to your suit? And look at your face. What happened? And your shoe. Have you been in a fight again? Police inspectors are not supposed to get in fights. That's a job for PCs, you told me. Where was this? Haven't I said you're too old for all that nonsense? That's what children do in the playground. Not grown men. And what have you done to your chin? You haven't been through town looking like this, have you? I hope nobody saw you. Get that suit off. I'll get it to the cleaners. Are you hurt anywhere? One of these days this job is going to get you killed. I wish you'd been a school teacher or a . . . *anything* but this dangerous carry on. Every day you walk out the door I'm left wondering if I'll even see you again.'

Mary's eyes became moist and she stuck a hand in her apron.

Angel produced a handkerchief from his pocket. She silently took it as he put his arms round her.

She wiped her eyes and hung onto the handkerchief.

Angel kissed her gently. 'You mustn't make more of this than it is. It was just a skirmish, Mary. That man Velleman wanted to see me.'

'You've told me about him.' She shuddered. 'He's a monster. A murderer.'

'I'll get him one day,' Angel heard himself say.

'I'm so scared, love,' Mary said.

Angel nodded. 'Well, Velleman made a proposal. I turned him down outright and he didn't like it. That's all.'

'So he started the fight?'

'Well, no. The fight was before. Now . . . how about we forget all this and sit down for dinner.'

Mary frowned. She clearly wanted to say more, but left it unspoken. 'Dinner's not ready just yet,' she said gently. 'You've time for a quick shower.'

He smiled at her. 'Mary, you're a mind reader.'

THREE

Bromersley town centre, South Yorkshire
Friday, 9 April, 10.30 a.m.

It was the following day, and PCs Sean Donohue and Martin Green were parked in a patrol car in a prominent position in Bromersley town centre. The town was busy with shoppers.

A young man was ambling around, chewing gum, hands in pockets, kicking a lager can along the street, when he spotted the police car.

He grinned and to the annoyance and inconvenience of shoppers, he dribbled the lager can to the front of the police car then gave it a powerful kick towards the radiator grill of the car. There was the sound of breaking glass as it fell onto the road.

PC Donohue couldn't get out of the car fast enough. His face was scarlet. 'Do you realise what you've done?'

Fluke stood there, hands still in pockets, chewing and grinning. 'Yeah. Scored the winner.'

Donohue examined the damage. 'That was deliberate.'

'Of course it was. I wouldn't want anybody to think it was a fluke,' he laughed. 'That's my name, Sydney Fluke.'

'You're coming down to the station.'

'I expect you'll want a statement,' Fluke said, pushing another piece of gum into his mouth.

'Get in the car,' Donohue snapped.

* * *

30 Park Street, Forest Hill Estate, Bromersley, South Yorkshire
Monday, 12 April, 5.10 p.m.

Three days later, Mary Angel returned from the post office to find the back door of their bungalow slightly ajar. At first she thought her husband had returned home early from work, but seeing no car in the open garage told her otherwise.

Somebody could be in the house. Maybe more than one person.

A shiver ran down her back.

She withdrew quickly and silently made her way back up the garden path and into the quiet street. She crossed the road, stood behind a parked car and waited.

She checked in her purse for her keys and gave a sigh of relief when she found them. Then she took out her mobile and rang her husband.

'Hello, Mary. Are you all right?'

'Can you come straightaway, Michael? I think there might be somebody in our house. I've just come back from the shop and the back door is ajar.'

'Stay right away from the house. Don't let anybody know you're around. Keep your eyes open. I'm on my way.'

Mary sighed. She put the phone back into her purse and looked back across the road at her garden path.

Minutes later, a police car pulled up in front of the house, its blue lights flashing. Two young patrolmen jumped out carrying their truncheons. They glanced round the street, looked over the bungalow and garden, saw Mary and waved.

Mary was sure she recognised one of them — a fresh-faced constable named Sean Donohue. She waved eagerly back at them from behind the parked car and breathed out slowly, shocked to hear her breath come out in a sudden sob of relief.

She watched them race through the open garden gate, down the garden path and round the corner of the bungalow to the back door.

A minute or so later, she saw her husband's car come into view. He flashed his lights as saw her, waved and drove straight into the open garage. Then he went quickly down the path to the back of the house.

Mary didn't like being kept out of the action. She wondered if they had caught anybody. After a few more minutes, she went across the road and up to the garden gate. She was no frail petunia when it came to standing up to people. It was her home, and she wanted to know — indeed she felt entitled to know — what the three men had found. They must have found somebody or something for them to take so much time.

She made up her mind. She threw open the garden gate and strode determinedly down the path. As she reached the rear corner of the bungalow she heard a voice through the open door.

'Thanks again, sir,' she heard one of the patrolmen say. 'We'll be on our way.' Then he opened the back door.

The other patrolman was with him. They met Mary on the doorstep.

PC Donohue's mouth dropped open. His eyebrows shot up. 'Oh, Mrs Angel,' he said. 'Good afternoon.'

The other patrolman nodded and smiled at her, and then they both rushed quickly away.

Mary went into the kitchen.

Her husband came up to her and kissed her.

'Are you all right, love?'

'Better now you're here, darling.' She squeezed his hand. 'I assume you didn't find anybody, then?'

'No. There was nobody here when we arrived, but somebody has been in. That window at the back has been broken and there are scuff marks on the windowsill.'

Mary wasn't happy. She didn't like the idea of strangers rifling through her things. She went through to the dining room to see the damage. There were a few shards of glass to clear up, and she could probably remove the scuff marks with soap and water.

Angel said, 'I'll get a chap to put a new sheet of glass in tomorrow.'

'Has anything been taken?'

'Not that I can see. I don't think that's what this break-in was about.'

'My jewellery!' Mary exclaimed, and rushed into the bedroom. She didn't have much. She was wearing her best rings and earrings, as usual. The rest was costume jewellery.

Angel followed her in. 'Anything missing?'

'No, it's not been touched,' she said.

Angel looked around and shook his head. 'Why would somebody break into a house in broad daylight and then apparently take nothing?'

He was trying to hide it, but Mary could see he was rattled.

* * *

A & E, General Hospital, Bromersley, South Yorkshire
Tuesday, 13 April, 11 a.m.

Angel was seated in the waiting room. He had his head tilted back and was gazing at the ceiling. He frequently looked at his watch and sighed noisily.

Angel wouldn't have bothered with A & E. It was his boss, Detective Superintendent Harker, who had made him attend, following Angel's casual report to him that a taxi had accidentally run over his foot.

It had happened while he was trying to assist the driver to park next to his car, in a road where there was very limited space. The taxi driver was very apologetic but no permanent harm was done. And Angel was the first to admit that it was partly his fault and he would be happy to forget the whole incident. It had been embarrassing more than anything, especially in front of the small crowd of passers-by who had stopped and offered to help. It wasn't worth all that fuss.

A nurse came to the department door with a clipboard.

Angel straightened up and looked at her.

She glanced down at the clipboard. 'Michael Angel?'

Surprised, he breathed out heavily, held up a hand and began to stand up.

'This way.' She set off down the corridor, leaving Angel to limp along behind.

She reached a cubicle and he followed her in. She drew the curtain and looked at the clipboard again. 'Now, a car ran over your right foot?'

'Yes,' he said.

'Were you wearing these shoes?'

'Yes.'

'Take off your shoe and sock. Does it hurt?'

'No . . . Well . . . Certain parts hurt if you press hard, but it doesn't hurt much.'

'A bit bruised. Hmm. Wait here,' she said, and whisked through the curtain like Madam Arcati.

After a short time, the nurse appeared with a young woman in an unbuttoned white coat and a stethoscope round her neck.

The doctor looked at Angel's foot. 'Can you walk all right?' she said. 'No pain?'

Angel confirmed that the accident had left him with no severe pain and that he had no difficulty in walking.

'Could have damaged the soft tissue,' the doctor said. She turned to the nurse. 'Have it X-rayed.'

Then she smiled at Angel. 'I don't think there's anything to worry about. Come and see me tomorrow. Make an appointment with the nurse.' Then she fought her way through the curtains and was gone.

* * *

DI Angel's office, Bromersley Police Station, South Yorkshire
Friday, 16 April, 10 a.m.

Angel was dealing with an accumulation of several days' post, neglected because more important matters had pressed upon him, when there was a knock on the door.

It was DC Edward Scrivens. 'Excuse me, sir. I've got Sam Spinetti here.'

Angel raised his eyebrows. 'Slippery Sam?' He swivelled the office chair round to see him. 'Yes, Ted.'

Angel knew him well. Spinetti came from Dublin many years ago, a small man, now in his seventies, who looked as innocent as a newborn babe. He was, though, a well-known pickpocket and thief.

'He's been accused of stealing a woman's purse from out of her shopping basket in the market, sir,' Scrivens said. 'When I searched him he also had two wallets that weren't his in his pocket. He said he wanted to see you because he had something to tell you that you would want to hear. Have you time to see him?'

'What has he got to say for himself?'

'Oh, he's not denying the charges, sir.'

'All right. Bring him in.'

Scrivens went out and returned a moment later with Spinetti.

'Come in, Sam,' Angel said. 'You got caught again. When are you going to give it all up and retire?'

'That's my trouble, Mr Angel. It's the only thing I know about. It's what me dear old father taught me . . . and his father afore him. It's in me blood.' He looked up at the DC then back at Angel. 'Could I speak with you private, like — by yourself, on your own, just you and me, the two of us, by ourselves?'

Angel looked at Scrivens, and the young detective nodded.

'Come back in five minutes,' Angel said.

Scrivens went out.

Sam came up close to Angel, leaned over him and spoke in a whisper.

'I got a bit of information,' he said. 'Must be worth a tenner, Mr Angel.'

At the same time, using his two middle fingers, Sam dipped into Angel's jacket pocket, lifted his mobile phone out and palmed it as quickly as any Artful Dodger would have done.

Angel didn't seem to suspect a thing.

'Sit down,' the policeman said.

As Spinetti sat down, he casually transferred the mobile to the back of his knee.

Angel said, 'Sam, you know I don't pay the public's money out unless I get good value. I would have to be given the information first to fairly judge its value . . . whether it was worth a tenner or not.'

'Yes, sir. That's only right, sir,' Spinetti said as he slid the mobile down the back of his leg onto the carpet and concealed it by holding his foot lightly over it.

'Well, what is it?'

'Well now, you've just charged a geezer called William Hart with murder, haven't you, Inspector? It was in all the papers. Well, he was going round with Big Gloria, who used to be a singer. She's always round the clubs and the casinos. Her full name is Gloria Van Haven. She lives somewhere in Manchester . . . I don't know exactly where, but I could find out. They were very close — they lived together — until about a month ago, when they had a big row and split up. He left her, by all accounts. Now, Inspector Angel, is that worth a tenner or not?'

Angel scratched his head. He took out an envelope from his inside pocket and made a note. 'Tell me about Gloria Van Haven. How soon can you find out her address? And why did you call her *Big* Gloria? Is she six feet tall?'

'No. No. Big *up front*, Inspector,' he said indicating his own puny chest. 'You know.' He pursed his lips and nodded several times to emphasise the point.

Angel nodded in understanding and put the envelope away. 'And how about finding me her address?'

'Ah, well now, she used to sing in pubs,' Spinetti said as he gently nudged the mobile under Angel's desk out of sight. 'In the good old days, mind, when they was doing well. I'm sure there's many a landlord round here who would have her address from the old days.'

Angel wrinkled his nose and reached into his back pocket. He handed Spinetti a £20 note. 'It would have been fifty, Sam, if you could have given me her address.'

Spinetti took the note and pocketed it faster than a bullet.

There was a knock and Scrivens put his face round the door. 'Have you finished, sir?'

Spinetti chuckled. 'Yes, my man. You can take me to me private apartment.'

Scrivens took him back to his cell.

Angel resumed dealing with the post, and after hour or so the phone rang again. He reached out for it.

'Angel.'

It was a young woman's voice, loud and confident. 'Hey, you that detective that's sometimes in the papers? The one what they said, "Like the Mounties, he always gets his man"?'

'It was actually reported that *I* had said that, by a cub reporter who wanted a big headline for his piece. Anyway, what's your name and what can I do for you?'

'I wanna meet you, Michael Angel. I hear that you're straight and I can trust you. I got a deal I can put to you that you're gonna really like. My name's Gloria Van Haven. I've been with a man for over five years. Let's call him Mr V. He's high up in a gang of crooks: thieves and murderers. To tell the truth, after five long years, he's dropped me and picked up with a skinny young lass who's come into money. Well, I can tell you all about him and where you can pick him up. And I keep a daily journal. I've kept it since I first went out with him. It's about what I do and how I feel about it, but it also has references to all the jobs the gang's pulled.'

Angel said, 'I'll be in the station all day, you can call in—'

'No,' the woman broke in. 'He has his spies all over the place. It would have to be in a place with no people. I couldn't be seen with you. Perhaps away in the country where there's very little traffic. Erm . . . say halfway between the villages of Sevensee and Hollington. Do you know that area?'

'I know it.'

'There's a bridge, where the road goes over a railway line. I could meet you there . . . at noon . . . today.'

Then suddenly, in a hushed, urgent voice, she added, 'Got to go. Being watched. Please be there. *Please.*'

There was a click and the line went dead.

Angel looked at his watch. It was nearly eleven thirty. He reached for his hat.

* * *

The Cottage, Bottom Harvest Lane, Crossley, near Tunistone, South Yorkshire
Friday, 16 April, noon

A man walked along a quiet country road to an isolated house eight miles from Bromersley. There was a taxi parked on the drive.

The man opened the front gate, walked up the path and knocked on the door.

It was opened by a middle-aged man with the type of big moustache much favoured by the RAF at one time. He was putting on his suit jacket.

He smiled at the stranger. 'Yes? What can I do for you?'

'Are you Alfred Beecroft?' the stranger said.

'Yes. Why?'

'Are you a taxi driver?'

'Yes. Did you want a lift somewhere?' Beecroft said, then he noticed that the man was wearing surgical gloves.

'Are you alone?'

Beecroft thought that was a curious question. He wasn't at all happy with the situation. 'What do you want?' he said firmly.

The stranger didn't reply, instead he looked round the room as if he was taking stock.

Beecroft screwed up his face. This man was up to something.

Beecroft's heart began to beat faster.

'I'm on my way out to work,' he said firmly. 'You'll have to excuse me.'

He tried to pass the stranger but the man wouldn't move.

'*Excuse me!*' he said. His face reddened as he glared at the intruder.

The man pulled a small handgun from his pocket.

'You're not going anywhere,' he said, pointing the gun at Beecroft's chest.

The taxi driver swallowed even though his mouth was dry. He couldn't take his eyes off the gun. He moved slowly backwards through the doorway into the living room.

'What do you want?' he said. 'There's nothing here. I'm not a rich man.'

'I want your taxi.'

'Take it,' he said. 'You can have it. I'll give you the key.' He reached into his pocket and pulled out the black remote control. 'Here,' he said, and tossed it towards the man, at the same time making a lunge for the gun.

It went off.

Flakes of whitewash fluttered down from the ceiling.

Beecroft squeezed the gunman's wrist with both hands. Meanwhile, the man used his free hand to punch Beecroft round the head and face.

The onslaught was hurting Beecroft, but he wouldn't let go of the man's wrist and eventually managed to give it a mighty bang on the edge of the open door. The stranger dropped the gun. Beecroft put his foot on it and gave the man a mighty punch on the jaw which made him stagger backwards. Then Beecroft bent down to get the gun. Before he could pick it up, the stranger sprang forwards, pushed Beecroft halfway across the room, picked up the gun and fired it three times at the taxi driver, who went down like a log.

* * *

Sevensee Bridge, halfway between the villages of Sevensee and Hollington, near Tunistone, South Yorkshire
Friday, 16 April, noon

Meanwhile, Angel arrived at Sevensee Bridge. It was located on a straight open road, so that he could see for some distance when a vehicle was coming towards him from the front, or in the mirror, coming from behind. It occurred to him he had no idea what Gloria Van Haven looked like or what kind of vehicle she might arrive in.

He looked round at the scenery. He opened the car window and looked at the scenery. The fields were a patchwork of every shade of green, with a few brown plots here and there.

He checked his watch. It was a quarter past twelve. He switched on the radio. Reception was bad. Unusual, but he was close to the Pennines. He tried other stations. Mostly distorted pop music. He turned it off.

He wondered if there was anything interesting happening at the station. He reached in his jacket pocket for his mobile. It wasn't there. He checked his other pockets. It wasn't there either. He thought a moment or two. He couldn't remember using it that morning. It should have been in his pocket and it simply wasn't. It was possible he had left it on his desk . . .

He leaned across and switched on the radio phone. He pressed the first preset. Through the speaker he heard it dial out. After a while it was answered and the receptionist said, 'Bromersley Police. Can I help you?'

'Angel here. Can I speak to—'

But he was interrupted by the receptionist, who spoke over him and repeated, 'Bromersley Police. Can I help you?'

'Yes. It's DI Angel. Can—'

'Bromersley Police. Can I help you?'

He could hear her, but she couldn't hear him.

He heard her mutter, 'Oh it's one of *them*.' And then there was silence.

Angel looked at his watch. It was half past twelve.

FOUR

Side door, Bromersley Building Society, Coal Street, Bromersley, South Yorkshire
Friday, 16 April, 12.30 p.m.

On the dot of half past twelve a taxi drove up to the side door of the Bromersley Building Society. The driver parked and went into the main entrance. He approached the reception desk and asked the young lady to let the manager know that the taxi he had ordered had arrived.

The driver returned to his seat in the taxi. From the mirror he could see them as they came: two clerks and a white linen bag with the words 'Bromersley Building Society' printed on it. The bag wasn't big, but it seemed heavy. They opened the taxi door, put the bag on the floor of the cab and then climbed in. When they were settled in their seats, one of them lifted the bag on to his knees.

The driver stayed in his seat. He slid open the reinforced security window behind him. 'Good afternoon, gentlemen. National Bank?'

'Yes, please,' one of them said.

The driver closed the security window, locked it and drove the taxi towards the National Bank. He was there in two or three minutes, but drove quickly past it.

The clerks called out, telling him he was going the wrong way. He ignored them. One of them left his seat, tried to open the security window, even banged it with his shoe but they couldn't stop him. They didn't even crack the glass.

He drove faster and faster for about two minutes, out to the ring road, and then turned off down a country lane that led to a copse. He stopped, put on a black balaclava and pulled out his gun. He opened the security window behind him and pointed the gun at them.

They were crouching by the security window because of the limiting height of the taxi. Then they saw the gun.

One of them said, 'Oh my God!'

'Pass me the bag,' the driver said.

The one holding the bag said, 'No.'

The driver fired a shot into upholstery of the back seat.

'Next bullet will be for you,' the driver said.

'Give it to him, Brian.'

Brian hesitated then lifted up the bag and passed it through the security window. The man took it and put it in the cab beside him.

'Now, both of you,' he said, 'empty your pockets.'

Brian, clearly the braver of the two clerks, said, 'What for?'

The driver held the gun more tightly. 'Because I say so. Hurry up.'

The two clerks piled the respective contents of their pockets in small piles on the seats. Each pile included a mobile phone.

'Right,' he said. 'Now get out.'

The two clerks scrambled out of the taxi. They couldn't get out quickly enough.

Then the driver engaged gear, let in the clutch, and the taxi roared away. As he drove, he dragged the balaclava off over his head. He soon reached the ring road, and drove along it for a few hundred yards before turning off directly into the huge car park of Cheapo's the supermarket. He chose a space in the middle of the car park, near to where he had parked his own car earlier that day. He quickly transferred the linen bag from the cab of the taxi to the boot of his car and drove away.

* * *

Meanwhile, back at the police station, Detective Superintendent Harker's telephone rang.

It was the station's telephone receptionist. 'There's a man on the phone urgently asking for DI Angel. He says he wants to report a murder and a robbery. I can't raise the DI on his office phone nor on his mobile. They know nothing in the detectives' room. Have you any idea where he might be?'

Harker wrinkled his nose. 'No, I haven't, miss. Put him through to me. I'll have to speak to him.'

* * *

Sevensee Bridge, near Tunistone, South Yorkshire
Friday, 16 April, 12.45 p.m.

Angel was still patiently waiting by Sevensee Bridge. A tractor had passed him, and two cars. None of them stopped or even glanced at him. But then, he saw a large silver car approaching quite fast. He thought it was a Daimler.

As it came nearer, he could see that it was being driven by a woman.

This could be Gloria Van Haven. If it was, she was about forty-five minutes late. However, the car wasn't slowing down, and seconds later it flew past, ignoring him completely.

It seemed Gloria Van Haven simply wasn't coming. Angel decided he had waited long enough. It had all been a waste of time. Maybe there would be a message for him in his office when he returned.

He switched on the engine, turned the car round and made his way quickly back to Bromersley.

The journey was uneventful. He arrived in Bromersley at about 1.15 p.m. As usual he parked the BMW in his allocated space at the back of the building. He shoved his key card in the lock of the station's rear door. The door opened, and he passed the cells and went along the corridor to his office. 'Excuse me, sir,' a hesitant voice called him just as he reached his door. It was Cassandra Jagger, the young police cadet who'd been covering reception. She seemed embarrassed and awkward. 'I've been looking all over for you.'

'I've been out,' he said. 'What's the matter?'

'The super wants to see you,' she said, lowering her eyes. 'He says it's very urgent.'

Angel's face wrinkled. He didn't see eye to eye with his superior. 'Right, Cassie. I'll go up straight away.'

She smiled and turned away.

'Oh, Cassie? Are there any other messages?'

'No, sir.'

'Ask around, will you? I'm expecting one.'

'Yes, sir.'

He turned up the corridor and soon came to the door with the words 'Detective Superintendent Horace Harker' painted on it. He braced himself for trouble, breathed in deeply, knocked on the door and went in.

As expected, the smell was something between a chemist's dispensary and a knocking shop.

The superintendent was aged about fifty-five. He was a skinny man with very little hair. Angel thought he looked like a skull with two big ears.

The desk was piled high with papers, stationery, copies of the *Police Gazette*, and every kind of cold medicine under the sun. Angel even noticed a woollen tartan sock peeking out from under a mound of papers. There was also the constant whirring of two portable electric fan heaters directed towards his feet.

'Been looking for you,' Harker said. 'Rang your landline, your mobile, and sent a girl running round looking for you. You weren't in, and nobody knew where you were. Just had a report of a robbery from Bromersley Building Society. Almost a quarter of a million pounds in used notes and some silver. You not being about, I sent DS Carter. Now get on with it.'

‘Right, sir,’ Angel said. ‘Anything else?’

‘No. What you hanging about for? Expecting a medal?’

As always, Angel didn’t reply to the jibe. If he had, he would have initiated the beginning of the end of his career as a policeman.

He closed the door. He saw a plastic cup from the tea machine on the floor and kicked it with all his might down the corridor, and then three times more all the way to his office door. There, he stopped and exhaled a lungful of air. Then he picked the cup up, went into his office and put it in the bin.

Cassie saw him and followed him in. He had a face like thunder.

He looked at her. His face brightened expectantly.

‘I asked around and there are no other messages for you,’ she said.

The muscles of his face tightened.

‘Righto, Cassie.’

She went out.

Whatever had happened to that woman, Gloria Van Haven? Angel frowned. He spent a few moments thinking about what might have happened when he heard the familiar ring of his mobile phone. He traced the sound to under his desk but couldn’t see it. He pushed the desk a few centimetres forward and there it was on the carpet, ringing its head off. He snatched it up.

‘Angel,’ he said into the mouthpiece. It was DS Carter.

‘Now then, Flora. What’s happened?’

She gave him a potted account on the facts of the case, ending with a report that the regular driver of the taxi and the taxi itself were missing.

‘The boss of Rocket Taxis is very worried,’ she said.

‘I’ll have a word with them. See what I can find out.’

‘Right, sir.’

He cancelled the call and after locating the number, dialled Rocket Taxis. He was soon speaking to Reg Bush, the proprietor.

‘Alfred Beecroft has been with me for twelve years,’ Bush said. ‘He’s the most reliable driver I’ve got. He had a pickup at Bromersley Building Society this morning. Same job he always does. Except this time he never made it there. A stranger turned up instead. That’s what I heard from two of the clerks behind the desk. I mean, they thought it was weird, but this guy was driving one of my taxis. So they let it slide.’

‘And Alfred himself?’ Angel cut in. ‘You’ve had no contact — heard nothing from him?’

‘Not a peep.’ Bush’s voice was weary. ‘You think you know somebody . . . but now both him and my taxi have gone AWOL.’

‘We’re doing everything we can to find them, Mr Bush,’ Angel said. ‘But I have to ask — did you notice anything different about Alfred’s behaviour lately?’

A silence followed. Then, ‘Nothing I noticed,’ Bush answered at last. ‘Why — you don’t think *Alfred* could be in on this?’

‘It’s too early to say for certain, Mr Bush,’ Angel replied. ‘But tracking him down is our top priority right now.’ He took Alfred Beecroft’s home address, which was in the hamlet of Crossley, and the taxi’s number plate and closed the call.

He went straight out to his car and drove quickly to Crossley, then to Bottom Harvest Lane and to the only building there, the Cottage. Its name was on the garden gate.

He stopped the car in the lane at the front of the cottage and went up the path. He went up to knock on the door but it wasn’t closed completely. It swung open and there on the living room floor was the body of a man. He was sporting a big, black, RAF-type moustache. His eyes were staring at the ceiling. His mouth gaped open to reveal a set of top dentures, which had slipped down and were resting on his bottom lip. *Dentures*. Angel suppressed a shudder at the sight of them on so young a man. There was a patch of coagulated blood around his stomach.

Angel had not touched anything, nor did he intend to.

He returned to the car.

Despite his appearance, Angel thought that he knew the man from somewhere. Then he remembered. It was only a few days ago. This was the man who accidentally ran over his foot. It was the big moustache that had made him so memorable.

When he was settled in the driver's seat, he closed his eyes for a few moments. These awful sights never leave you. They burn themselves into your memory and stay there.

He finally took out his mobile and called DS Carter.

'Flora,' he said. 'I'm at the missing taxi driver's cottage. He's dead. Looks like he's been shot.' He gave her the address.

'Oh, sir, I was afraid of that,' she said. 'Yes. Of course. I think I've about finished here.'

'As you've finished, would you advise Dr Mac?'

'Yes, sir. And I'll see you myself in about forty-five minutes.'

He ended the call and scrolled down his phone directory, tapping on the button that would dial the duty sergeant at Bromersley Police Station.

'Duty officer, Sergeant Clifton,' the no-nonsense voice said.

'Angel here, Bernie. I'm at a murder scene at Crossley, near Tunistone. Advise SOC and Don Taylor, will you?'

'Hold on, sir. Let me tell him now. It'll save a minute or two.'

Angel heard him walk out of the charge room.

'Don, I've got the DI on the line,' he said. 'He's at a murder scene. He wants you there ASAP. I'll give you the address in a minute.'

'Right.'

The sergeant came back to the phone. 'He's getting his team ready, sir.'

'Right, Bernie. There's something else. Very important. I need to find a missing taxi. Probably taken by our murder suspect earlier today. I expect they'll have abandoned it by now. That taxi could be bursting with vital evidence. Will you notify the two local radio stations, our patrols and

Sheffield, Rotherham and Doncaster forces to look out for it, to isolate it and guard it for us until we can get to it? And if anybody spots it, please put them onto me.'

'Yes, sir. Can I have a description of the vehicle?'

'Of course.'

He gave him the number and a description of the taxi and the address of the murdered man. 'There's something else, Bernie. Will you give me the number of Manchester central police station?'

'Of course, sir. I have it handy, somewhere.' He found it.

Angel wrote it in his notebook and ended the call.

The he redialled Reg Bush of Rocket Taxis.

'Mr Bush, it's DI Angel. I'm very sorry to have to tell you that Alfred Beecroft is dead. Can you tell me if he had any relatives living round here?'

'Oh dear. Quite a shock,' Bush said. 'Not that I know of. I saw him every day. I knew him quite well . . . He never spoke of anybody. He lived by himself and seemed perfectly content. What did he die of?'

'Erm . . . we don't know, yet. Foul play, I'm afraid. Do you know of anybody who would want to kill him?'

'Nobody. Alfred was one of the nicest men in the world. One of those men it would be hard to fall out with. Reliable, honest and straightforward.'

'I'm sorry for your loss.'

'Thank you,' Bush said.

'I'll get back to you,' Angel said. He ended the call and immediately rang the Manchester number.

He was quickly put through to a DI. 'Good afternoon. My name is DI Harris. Is that *the* Michael Angel from Bromersley?'

Angel smiled. It was nice to be recognised. 'Yes, and thank you for taking my call. I'm just following up a vague tip-off by an informer. It involves a character called Gloria Van Haven. I understand she was a singer in pubs a few years ago and can still be seen holding court in night clubs and casinos in or around Manchester. Do you know of her?'

'Yes, we know of her. But nothing official. She's not been in any trouble that we know of. She's a bit of a local celebrity. I personally don't go to casinos for . . . recreation. Not on a detective inspector's pay. So I've never seen her, but it's rumoured that she's very well off and spends time at Lola's nightclub and casino. The manager there is called James Robertson. If you speak to him he should be able to help you.'

* * *

Forty-five minutes later, the SOC van arrived at the cottage with the team led by DS Don Taylor.

Angel was still in his car. He lowered the window.

'Good afternoon, sir,' Taylor said. 'Do you know who found him?'

'I did, Don,' Angel said. 'Nothing's been touched.'

'That makes a pleasant change, sir.'

The SOC team began to don their white overalls with covered footwear, hats and masks to begin their slow, gruesome work.

After taking many photographs, one of the team began to run a low-powered vacuum over the dead man.

About an hour later the pathologist, Dr Mac, arrived. He dressed up in a set of whites together with blue wellingtons and began examining the dead man in situ.

The mortuary van arrived shortly afterwards. Two men in blue theatre garb stood patiently waiting outside the house door with a crude-looking stretcher standing on its end.

From the car, Angel saw Dr Mac come out and speak briefly to the mortuary assistants. They went into the house with the stretcher. The doctor began the business of taking off his white overalls.

Angel got out of the car and went up the garden path to the pathologist.

'Hello there, Michael,' said Mac. 'Nasty business.'

'It's always a nasty business when you're called in. What have you got?'

'Do you know,' Mac said as he unzipped the front of his one-piece white suit, 'I knew you were going to ask me that . . . Three bullets in the stomach. Small calibre. Time of death . . . between eleven this morning and one this afternoon.'

Angel nodded. 'Thanks, Mac. Is that all?'

At that moment, one of the mortuary assistants came rushing up to Mac.

'Hey, Doctor. They've found a handkerchief under the body. And it's been used. It's crumpled up. And it's got a letter on it. An initial. DS Taylor says it must have belonged to the suspect.'

Mac blinked. 'Thanks, John,' the doctor said. 'That's great. Might be able to get DNA from it.'

The man ran off to spread the news elsewhere.

'That'll make my job easy then,' Angel said.

Mac threw the white suit in the back of his car. 'I wonder what the letter is?'

'Don't rush off, Mac. I'll find out.'

Angel went down to the front door of the cottage and called in, 'Anybody there know what the letter on the handkerchief you've found is?'

A voice cried out, 'Yeah. It's W.'

* * *

About an hour later, around 9 p.m., Angel's mobile rang. It was the night duty officer at Bromersley station.

'We've had a report that the missing taxi has been found in the Cheapo's car park, sir,' he said. 'I've sent a patrol car there to check it out.'

'Oh, good.' Angel said. 'Hopefully there'll be valuable evidence there. It'll need taping and guarding until SOC can get to it in the morning.'

'I'll see to that, sir.'

Angel told Don Taylor the good news.

'More overtime, sir,' the sergeant said. 'I can do with the money. You don't get overtime, do you, sir? That's rough.'

Angel smiled. 'I don't mind. My wife's sister and her two kids are down from Edinburgh for the weekend. Gets me out of that.'

Taylor nodded and smiled. 'I think we've just about finished here. Is there any evidence that the murderer used the bathroom at all?'

'No, Don, but you must check it out.'

'Right, sir. We'll pack up for the night, and I'll send two of the team down here tomorrow to finish off while we see to the taxi.'

'I may as well go home,' Angel said. He looked at his watch. It was almost midnight.

'We won't be long behind you. Goodnight, sir,' he said.

Angel got into the BMW and drove away. It was a lovely night and there was little traffic on the road, so he made good time. As he reached Park Street, he could see that his own bungalow was in darkness except for the bedroom light. Mary was still awake, though their visitors were already tucked up in bed.

He put the BMW in the garage, pulled down the door and was locking it when he heard a shuffling noise coming from the back of the bungalow.

Somebody was there. It wasn't likely to be Mary.

He crept silently across the corner of the lawn in time to see the silhouette of a big figure running powerfully across the far end of the lawn, over a low privet fence, onto the pavement and away.

Angel felt a wave of anger wash over him at the sight of yet another unwanted guest snooping round his property in the night.

He unlocked the back door and switched on the yard light. Everything outside seemed in order. There wasn't much there. Four wheelie bins, a clothes line and a metal dish with a drop of milk in that Mary had put out for any passing stray cat.

He switched off the outside light, closed the door, and locked and bolted it.

He didn't see the antique Rolls-Royce gliding past the end of the street.

FIVE

30 Park Drive, Forest Hill Estate, Bromersley, South Yorkshire
Saturday, 17 April, morning

Angel didn't work on Saturdays unless something needed his attention . . . or because his wife's relations were visiting . . . or simply because he couldn't keep away. He knew that Don Taylor and some of the SOC team would be examining the stolen taxi, and he had more than a casual interest in what they might find. Taylor had organised an eight-wheel low loader to collect the taxi and move it to the station garage to make it more secure and convenient to work on.

Angel drove to the police station and called at reception for the day's post. He was handed the usual bundle of letters and packets held together by an elastic band. He looked through the post for anything of interest. There was an unusual envelope addressed to the chief constable. Unusual because it was computer-printed, didn't have a stamp and wasn't franked. It must have been delivered by hand. He didn't open that, of course, but he opened all the other post that was not specifically addressed to a particular person or rank. It was all unusually very humdrum. He dropped it into his out tray until Monday.

He sauntered out of the building by the back door into the vehicle impound. He passed the closed vehicle examination bay doors and went up to a side door that opened onto a large area, where stood the taxi on a ramp. He went in and found three SOC officers in white clothing working on it.

They looked round at him when he closed the heavy door. It made a loud noise, which echoed around the room. It could not be closed quietly.

Angel stood back and watched the activity. He didn't want to interfere and slow the examination down. After a few moments, DS Taylor came across to him.

'Found anything of interest, Don?' Angel said.

'We've found a shell case from a thirty-eight under the driver's seat, sir,' Taylor said. 'We've not yet found where the bullet landed. According to one of the victims, it was somewhere in the back of the car.'

'Too early to ask if there was a fingerprint on it?' Angel said.

'Yes,' Taylor said. 'But Ballistics might already be familiar with the gun that fired it.'

Angel nodded. 'When you've checked it for prints, will you send it to them? Let's hope that we get something from them quickly.'

'Yes, sir.'

Angel looked at his watch. 'Must go.'

He returned to his office and looked at his 'must do' list. Almost everything had been crossed off, but one of the items still there was 'Contact Gloria Van Haven'. It was followed by a Manchester phone number, for Lola's nightclub.

Angel tapped it out on his landline.

It was answered by a man. 'Yeah?'

'Is that Lola's?' Angel said.

'Yeah. What do you want? We're closed. We don't open until eight o'clock tonight. Do you want to reserve a table . . . or something?'

'No, thank you,' Angel said. 'This is DI Angel of Bromersley Police. Can I speak to Mr James Robertson?'

'I'm afraid he's not here,' said the voice at the end of the line. 'I'm just one of the cleaners. Can I help you at all?'

'I'm trying to find the phone number of Miss Gloria Van Haven.'

'I'm sorry, but I can't help you there,' the voice said.

Angel heard a click at the end of the line and knew the conversation was over.

* * *

Meanwhile, over in the manager's office at Lola's nightclub, James Robertson placed the phone back in its cradle.

He'd made a quick decision in conversation with that detective.

I'm just one of the cleaners. As lies went, it was plausible enough. And no one could prove any different.

* * *

Manager's office, Lola's nightclub, Manchester
Saturday, 17 April, 11.30 p.m.

James Robertson, in a dinner jacket and white bow tie was alone in his office sitting at his desk. There were several piles of banknotes in front of him, and he was busy counting another.

The phone rang. He reached out for it.

'Yeah . . . Who? . . . Put him through . . . Hello, Mr Starr . . . When . . . As soon as that? . . . I understand, Mr Starr . . . Tell the boss it'll be done. I'll see to it personally.'

He ended the call then tapped in a number. It was soon answered. 'Send Sebastian and Hans to my office immediately.'

He resumed counting the money, then he put the notes together in one pile, put an elastic band around it and stood up.

On the wall behind the desk was a large erotic photograph of a woman wearing a couple of powder puffs. He pulled the edge of the picture frame towards him. It opened to reveal a wall safe. He entered the combination and opened the door.

At that moment there was a knock at the door.

Robertson froze.

'Who is it?' he called.

'Sebastian.'

'Just a minute,' he called.

Robertson put the money in the safe, closed it and replaced the picture. He glanced at his desk, then round the room to make sure everything was in order, checked the handgun in his waistband, then went to the door, unlocked it and pulled it open.

Sebastian looked at him and blinked.

'Come in,' Robertson said to the big man. 'Is Hans with you?'

'Yeah.'

Hans was sauntering up behind Sebastian. The two heavies ambled into the office.

Robertson returned his desk. 'Well, come on in . . . both of you. And shut the door.'

When the two heavies were standing in front of him, he said, 'I will be wanting you to dispose of . . . a big package later tonight. I want it to be done quickly and discreetly. You understand?'

'Yeah. Is it a he or a she?' Hans said.

Robertson scowled. He had thin lips and a cruel mouth. 'What's it matter? It'll be an *it*. You can take *it* rolled in that rug you're standing on . . . but bring the rug back. You can carry it out of here, along down this corridor and out through the emergency fire door, as before. Park the car near the door. It can all be done in thirty seconds if you're quick. All right?'

The two men nodded.

Then he looked at Hans and Sebastian and in a quieter tone said, 'Right. Wait in the staff room. Keep your traps shut. I'll ring you when I want you. Now, I'm very busy, so get out.'

The men nodded again and trundled out of the office.

Robertson followed them up to the door and turned the key once more. Then he returned to his desk and put some papers away in a drawer, leaving the desktop clear. From his jacket pocket he produced a small roll of white linen, which he opened out onto the desk. It held seven or eight scalpels with different cutting heads, blades, retractors and surgical scissors. He selected one scalpel, held it up to the light, nodded, smiled and put it down on the desk top, then rolled up the fabric and put it back in his pocket. From another pocket he took out a slim envelope, tore it open and took out a pair of rubber gloves. It took a little while to put them on because they were skin tight.

There was a knock at the door.

'Who is it?'

'It's me,' a gentle female voice said.

Robertson felt a dark shudder of excitement in his chest that spread to the rest of his body.

He smiled. 'I'm coming, Gloria.'

* * *

Chief constable's office, Bromersley Police Station, South Yorkshire
Monday, 19 April, 8.30 a.m.

The chief constable's secretary came into his office with a handful of papers.

'I've done the post, Mr MacAndrews,' she said. 'I didn't open this one. It's marked "Private and Confidential".'

MacAndrews took the envelope from her. It had computer-printed name and address on a white envelope, and there was no stamp.

He picked up his paper knife and slit the envelope open. It read . . .

17 April

For the urgent attention of the chief constable

The reason there is so much crime is because the police is full of so-called respectable officers who are bent.

For instance, the murder of that taxi driver yesterday and the robbery of the building society was executed by your much-praised but covertly dishonest DI Angel. But don't take my word for it. Ask him where he was at the time of the murder. Also, I suggest you suspend him from work, otherwise he'll begin to cover up his tracks.

MacAndrews gave an exasperated scoff. He turned the letter over to see if there was any more. There wasn't.

'Oh! I do hate anonymous letters,' he said to himself. 'Especially when they're such blatant rubbish.'

He pressed a key on the communication box on his desk. 'Horace, come in here,' he said.

'Right, sir.'

Detective Superintendent Harker's office was next door, so he was there almost instantly.

MacAndrews gave him the letter to read.

'What do you want me to do, sir?' Harker said. 'We can't ignore it.'

'I don't suppose we can. Well, check out Angel's alibi and see if it's watertight.'

Harker sniffed. 'Right sir, I'll have Angel in.'

MacAndrews nodded and tried, and failed, to sound enthusiastic. 'Yes,' he said. 'It's the right thing to do, of course. Then we can file the thing and forget it. Do it now, Horace. And let me know how you get on,' he added.

'Yes, sir.'

'And let me know the distance between the place where Angel *says* he was and the scene of Beecroft's murder.'

Harker pursed his lips. 'It would be about fifteen miles. I know that area well.'

'Fifteen miles? He could do that in twenty minutes.'

'Less on a good day, sir . . . even on country roads,' Harker said.

'Interesting,' MacAndrews said slowly.

* * *

Three minutes later, Angel was in Harker's office reading the anonymous letter. He read it twice before sighing deeply then handing it back across the littered desk.

Angel ran his hand through his hair and eventually spoke. 'I don't know what to say, sir. It's not true, of course. I have no idea who could have made such an allegation.'

'The chief constable and I *know* that, Angel,' Harker said. 'Well, obviously the question is where were you at the time of the murder of that poor taxi driver?'

'I was out in the country at Sevensee Bridge. I was meeting a woman who was witness to—'

'So *she* can vouch for you, then?' Harker said. 'Good. What's her name?'

'No, she can't,' he said. 'She didn't turn up.'

Angel began to realise that he didn't have an alibi for that time.

'I didn't see *anybody*,' Angel said.

Harker's jaw dropped. 'You must have seen somebody . . . passers-by?'

'No,' Angel said. 'A few vehicles . . . cars, and a tractor, but nobody I knew. I didn't talk to anybody. Nobody stopped. There wasn't anybody.'

'How long were you there?'

'Too long. Dr Mac said death was between eleven and one. If you took the middle point between those times, it would be noon. Well, I arrived at Sevensee Bridge at about that time. I left my office to go and meet the witness at about eleven thirty and got back at around one fifteen. There would probably be personnel around the station who could support those times, I hope.'

'I hope so, too. While you were waiting, did you make any phone calls or receive any?'

'I didn't have my phone with me.'

Harker licked his bottom lip. 'What's the point of having a mobile phone if you don't have it with you?'

'Normally I do, but it seemed to have dropped off the desk in my office.'

'But you had the RT in the car. Didn't you think of using it?'

'Yes sir, I did. But Sevensee Bridge is in a valley. Reception was very bad. I couldn't get a strong enough signal.'

'I don't understand why you didn't tell somebody about your meeting.'

'There wasn't much time. She rang about eleven thirty and arranged the meeting for noon . . . it took me half an hour to get there.'

Harker shook his head. 'This woman, Angel . . . the woman who was prepared to give you some information. Have you managed to contact her since?'

'No, sir. I have tried. She frequents a Manchester nightclub regularly, I'm told. I've tried to contact her there but without success.'

'Well, Angel, that seems to be your only way out of this. You must get her to confirm that she made an arrangement to meet you at Sevensee Bridge at noon last Friday, as you have said, and explain why she didn't keep the appointment. Get it in writing, for goodness sake. And you'd better be quick about it.'

* * *

Angel picked up his landline phone and dialled a number.

It was soon answered. 'Lola's nightclub.'

'James Robertson, please.'

'Speaking.'

'This is DI Angel of Bromersley Police.'

The speaker made no reply, so Angel continued, 'I understand you're the manager, Mr Robertson.'

When Robertson spoke again, his voice sounded different. Changed. 'I am. How can I help you?'

'I want to speak to a lady called Gloria Van Haven, who I understand regularly visits the nightclub.'

'She used to be a regular client, but she seems to have gone away. She *was* talking about having a holiday, but I don't know . . .'

'Do you have her address?'

'No, I don't, I'm sorry.'

'Her phone number?'

'No.'

'Could you put me in touch with any person or organisation that might be able to help me?'

'I'm afraid we weren't that close, Inspector.'

Angel frowned. This man Robertson was remarkably unhelpful. He ended the call and immediately phoned Manchester Police. He eventually got through to DI Harris again.

'Harris, it's vitally important I contact Gloria Van Haven. We need a statement from her.'

'I'm sorry, Angel, but I just haven't the time and the men to devote to searching for witnesses for other forces. That's not *my* ruling. It's from the top. I'm sorry.'

Angel nodded. 'I understand. Then I want to advise you that I'll be coming into your jurisdiction to search for Gloria Van Haven myself later today.'

'That's fine. I'll report that, and I wish you very good hunting,' Harris said. 'I should start at the club itself . . . after nine o'clock. Many of the regulars will know Gloria, I would have thought. If you have any success, give me a call. You can phone me on my mobile.'

Harris gave Angel the number, which he put straight into his phone, then rang off.

* * *

Sydney Fluke was hanging around the front of the police station. He was being monitored on the security cameras, standing around looking thoughtful, head down, hands in pockets, slowly chewing gum and occasionally kicking invisible pebbles off the pavement into the road.

DS Carter had been alerted. She watched the CCTV monitor for a few minutes then went outside and spoke to him.

'Mr Fluke, is there something you want? I've been told that you've been hanging around here for some time.'

'It's a free country, isn't it?' he said. Then with his tongue he moved the chewing gum from one side of his mouth to the other. 'I can stand here if I want, can't I? It's not an offence, is it?'

'It certainly isn't if you're standing here innocently, but it *is* an offence if you are loitering with intent to commit a crime.'

'What if I stood *inside* the station? Would that be a crime?'

Flora looked at him strangely. 'Not if you were there on business, or had been taken there for questioning, or you were brought in as the result of an arrest order,' she said. 'Now, if I were you, I should just . . . quietly move along. Keep out of trouble.'

She turned and walked swiftly back to the door.

Fluke called after her, 'I do have some business to discuss with the police. I want to make a statement.'

She ignored him. She opened the station door, walked in and closed it.

Of all things, Sydney Fluke could not tolerate being ignored. That was the last straw.

'I want to make a bloody statement!' he bawled.

His body tensed. His face went red. Heat flushed through his body. After a few seconds, hands in pockets, he strode determinedly towards the police station, opened the door and went inside.

There was a reception area with five or six desks behind a heavy glass and wood barrier.

Three young constables left their desks came up to him, ready for trouble. One of them said, 'What do you want, lad?'

Another said, 'He wants to look inside one of our cells.'

The others laughed.

That was another thing. Sydney Fluke could not stand being laughed at.

He looked between their grinning heads at a plain, apple-green wall with a clock at the centre of it, about five metres away and just reachable above the barrier.

'I came to make a statement,' Fluke said.

'You've tried that trick before,' one of the constables said.

Fluke glared at him. That was the last straw. At that, Fluke's body shook with rage and frustration. He took a step back towards the door, wide eyed, with spittle showing at the corners of his mouth, and with his pulse pounding in his ears, he said, 'Well, I've got a new trick for today.'

Then he stepped backwards yet another pace, took his hands out of his pockets and looked at the specially prepared egg in his right hand. He raised his arm and threw the egg overhand at the clock on the wall at the far side of the room.

It was a bullseye right in the middle of the dial.

The shell broke and a green, smelly slime began to creep down the clock onto the wall, emitting the nastiest of odours. He had spent weeks making that stink bomb from an egg, ammonia and onion, and he was proud of the abominable, sulphurous stench it had produced. He grinned, turned and ran out of the station.

He was promptly followed by the three young constables holding their noses. They easily caught up with him and brought him back grinning through the stinking reception area into the charge room, under the eye of the duty officer, Sergeant Clifton.

Through another door DS Carter came in with Angel.

Angel looked at Clifton. 'Will you let me talk to the accused, Bernie?'

Clifton made a gesture with his hand towards Fluke. 'Sir.'

The accused smiled and chomped on his gum. He folded his arms.

Angel said, 'Is it correct, Fluke, that you released a stink bomb in the station?'

Fluke looked round. There were five people in the room besides himself. He appreciated the size of the audience.

'Yeah, I did,' Fluke said. 'I made it myself . . . at home.'

Angel shook his head. 'Well, why release it here?'

Fluke looked round the room at everybody's faces. 'It's a bit of fun, isn't it?'

There was a stony silence.

'Was there some other reason? Do you want to make a statement?'

'You say *that* to me every time I come in here.'

'And *every* time we organise it, you cry off . . . without any explanation.' Angel sighed. 'You go before the magistrates tomorrow morning at ten o'clock. I'm sure they'll be pleased to see you again.'

Fluke grinned. 'I'm sure they will,' he said. 'Might put me on their Christmas list.'

Angel sighed, then turned to Sergeant Clifton and gave him a wave. 'Thank you, Bernie.' Then he went out, followed by DS Carter.

On the way down the corridor, Angel turned to Flora. 'There's something very strange about Fluke. He's committed three crimes in quick succession. The first two resulted in fines. And this latest one was pure stupidity. He doesn't seem to know when he's had enough. I don't quite know what the magistrates will do with him tomorrow morning.'

'What do you expect them to do, sir?'

Angel scratched his head. 'Anything from a psychiatric examination to ninety days inside. I just don't know what he's up to.'

SIX

Lola's nightclub, Manchester
Tuesday, 20 April, 9.00 p.m.

Angel found Lola's on a little side street off Bury New Road in Manchester. He parked the BMW and walked the hundred yards or so to the blinding lights displaying the name of the club and the flashing outline in strip lighting of a young man and woman dancing.

He went through all the necessary formalities of becoming a member, paid the fee, was given an admission card and went into the club.

The orchestra was playing a waltz. There were a few dancers. It didn't seem busy. He found the bar. A well-dressed, pleasant barman with a red face came over.

He ordered a whisky and soda, and as the barman dispensed the drink Angel asked, 'Do you know Gloria Van Haven?'

'Oh yes, sir. Everybody knows Miss Gloria.'

'Does she come here often? Do you think she'll be in tonight?'

The barman jerked his head backward. 'I really couldn't say, sir.'

Angel knew that whatever the barman knew about Gloria, he wasn't going to tell him anything more.

Angel paid him, then splashed some soda into his whisky and moved away to the end of the bar, taking the glass with him.

The tables were filling up. Near where he was standing, a middle-aged couple were being shown to a table by a waiter. The woman said something to her partner and then rushed away. Angel watched her pass the full length of the bar, then saw a black object on the floor behind her. She had dropped something. He walked over and picked it up. It was an evening dress purse. He looked around. She was nowhere to be seen. He took it to her partner, who was sitting at the table studying a large menu.

'Excuse me,' Angel said. 'The lady you're with . . . she dropped this.'

The man blinked. 'Oh? Yes, that *is* her purse. Thank you very much. Thank you very much, indeed.'

A moment later the lady who had dropped the purse appeared with a face like death. 'I've lost my purse, Clem. I don't—'

The man smiled at her and held it up.

She was clearly relieved.

He looked at Angel. 'This gentleman found it and kindly brought it to me.'

She smiled at Angel, looked at the glass he was holding, then at Clem, and said, 'Well, what are you waiting for, Clem? We must get the gentleman a drink!'

'I was waiting for you . . .'

'No,' Angel said. 'That's all right. I saw you drop it, that's all.' He turned away.

The lady caught his sleeve. 'Excuse me. This purse has all our money in it. We are most grateful. *What are you drinking?*'

He hesitated. 'Whisky and soda.'

The man said, 'Are you by yourself?'

'I am,' Angel said.

She said, 'You must join us. My name is Ann and my husband is Clement.'

Angel thought they were a wholesome enough couple, so he was pleased with their company, but it would in no way delay his effort to find Gloria, interview her and get back home to Mary.

Ann caught a passing waiter. 'Two glasses of house red and a whisky and soda, please.'

The waiter nodded, smiled and glided away.

Ann turned to Angel and pointed to a vacant chair next to hers. 'Please, sit down.'

'Thank you,' Angel said.

As he made the move, he saw the barman with the red face speaking into the phone on the bar and looking straight at him. When he saw Angel had seen him he instantly turned away.

Angel rubbed his chin. Things were happening.

Ann said, 'That's better.'

Angel said, 'Well . . . erm, thank you. Please, call me Michael. I'm trying to find a woman, I don't know if you know her? Gloria Van Haven.'

Ann's eyebrows went up. 'You're on a date . . . with *her*?'

'No. I'm a sort of . . . inquiry agent. Why? Do you know her?'

Clement said, 'Well, we know who you mean, and we've spoken to her, but it wouldn't be true to say we *know* her.'

Ann said, 'Don't quibble, Clem. We've met her. We've spoken to her. If she was passing we would exchange greetings, so we *know* her.'

Ann then looked at Angel. 'I think my husband means we don't know anything about her, except that we've heard she's very rich.'

Clement nodded. 'All right, then. We don't know anything *else* about her.'

Angel said, 'Does she come here every night? Will she be here tonight?'

Ann said, ‘Who knows? But she doesn’t come *every* night.’

‘Have you any idea where she lives?’ Angel said.

‘No,’ Ann said. She put her fingertips to her lips and frowned.

Clement said, ‘No, I’m sorry.’

Then Ann said, ‘But I know a woman who does.’

Angel’s eyes brightened.

She took out a mobile from the black purse and began scrolling and tapping.

Clem said, ‘Who are you ringing, love?’

Ann looked at Angel. ‘Well, when we were on holiday in Majorca, we met a woman who’s the wife of the man who used to make deliveries for a chemist in Upper Shelldale. She’ll know, because he used to deliver to Gloria Van Haven’s mother and other celebrities. He used to boast about it. She happened to tell me.’

The drinks arrived and Clement signed for them.

Ann’s phone was answered and an animated conversation took place between her and the lady in Upper Shelldale.

Angel and Clement sat there patiently waiting, glancing at the menus and occasionally sipping their drinks.

Eventually Ann finished the call. ‘Sorry, Michael. She and her husband have since split up and she doesn’t know or care where he’s got to. All I can tell you is that she definitely lives in Upper Shelldale.’

Angel smiled. ‘Thanks very much, Ann.’ He wasn’t too disappointed. It was definitely progress. Years ago, as a humble constable, he had often found wanted people through leg work like this.

From the corner of his eye Angel saw that a big man in a dinner jacket, with a face like a pound of tripe, had come into the ballroom and was looking around. Angel knew instantly it was Sebastian. He caught Angel’s eye and came straight across.

Sebastian leaned down close to his ear and sniffed. ‘Excuse me, sir, but there’s an urgent telephone call for you.’

Through leaning forward, the man's coat eased slightly and Angel saw that Sebastian was carrying a handgun in a shoulder holster.

A warning bell began to ring in Angel's head. His stomach churned. He rubbed the back of his neck.

'The caller said it was urgent, sir,' Sebastian said with a sniff.

'Oh?' Angel looked at Ann and Clem. 'Will you excuse me?' he said as he got to his feet.

Sebastian said, 'If you would follow me, sir. You can take it in the manager's office.'

'Thank you.'

Angel's heart was thumping. His mind was whizzing through his options as fast as a computer. He knew he was walking into trouble. He reached up to his top pocket and switched on his miniature recording device.

Sebastian crossed the ballroom and went through a door behind a pillar. Angel followed him into a corridor behind the scenes where the offices were. There were more several doors ahead. On the nearest was printed the word 'Manager'.

Suddenly Angel stopped. 'Excuse me.'

Sebastian turned.

Angel put his left arm straight up above his shoulder in the direction of the ceiling. 'Can you put your arm up like this?'

Sebastian stared at him.

'Well, can you?' Angel said.

The man hesitated.

He was a good six centimetres taller than Angel.

Angel said, 'I don't think you can.' He looked up at his own hand. 'You can't reach higher than that.'

Sebastian was still thinking.

Angel then said, 'And if I put *both* arms up and stretch, I can almost reach the ceiling. You can't, of course. It's because of your illness, isn't it?'

The big man sniffed. 'What do you mean? What illness?'

Angel triumphantly said, 'You can't. I knew you wouldn't be able to.'

'Of course I can,' Sebastian said, and he put both arms up towards the ceiling.

'That's good. But you're not holding your arms quite right. I'll show you.' Angel then went up close to him. 'Look upwards. Keep looking up,' he said. 'Keep looking.'

Then Angel put his hand inside Sebastian's dinner jacket, and slipped the handgun out of the holster. It felt good. It was heavy because it was fitted with a silencer. He knew straight away that it was an old Walther PPK/S and that it held eight rounds.

He pointed the Walther at the middle of Sebastian's chest and stepped back two paces. 'Right, buster. Keep those hands up where they are, turn around and lead me to the office in front. And don't bother knocking. Let's walk in fast.'

The man gasped in anger. 'The boss won't like that.'

'Good,' Angel said. 'Do as *I* say. *I'm* holding a gun on *you*. He isn't.'

'OK.'

They reached the door.

'Press the handle, push it open and walk straight in,' Angel said. 'I'm right behind you.'

The door opened with a bang to reveal James Robertson at his desk.

Angel's eyes tracked all over the room. He had to be alert. But he had been trained for it.

Robertson looked up, amazed at seeing Sebastian with his arms raised and an apologetic look on his face. Behind him, Angel held a gun trained on his spine.

'What's all this?' Robertson said as he stood up. He was smartly dressed in a dinner jacket, bow tie and white linen gloves.

Angel said, 'Put your hands on the desk where I can see them. And don't make any quick moves. I'm liable to pull this trigger and blow your hand off.'

He jabbed Sebastian in the back. 'Lie down in the middle of that carpet over there. And put your hands on your head.'

Then he pointed the gun at the other man. 'Mr James Robertson, I presume. Come carefully from behind that desk. Now slowly, very slowly, take off your jacket.'

As Robertson began to disrobe, Angel saw the handle of a gun sticking out of his waistband.

'Well, well, well. What have we here? Now, Mr Robertson, listen carefully to what I tell you. Your life could depend on it. With the tips of your fingers, slowly lift that gun out of your waistband and throw it towards me. Don't try anything clever. I am aiming at your stomach and the safety catch is off.'

The gun landed at his feet.

Angel slowly picked it up and promptly recognised it as a Beretta Tomcat. Small but deadly. He held it in his left hand.

'Now, come and join your friend Sebastian,' Angel said. 'Come on. Hurry up. But put your head where his feet are and your feet . . . that's it. Now put your hands on your head. That's it.'

Angel found himself an easy chair. He pushed it around with his foot so he could see both men as well as the door. Then he relaxed into it.

'Now then, Mr Robertson,' Angel said, 'I take it the urgent phone call was just a ruse to get me here.'

There was no reply.

'Well, I'm here now. What did you want me for?'

Still there was no reply.

'Well, I'll tell you what I came here for. I need to see Gloria Van Haven. If she's not here, I need her address.'

No reply.

'I intend to get it.'

Angel put the Beretta on his lap, took out his mobile and called a number from his library.

'I'm not on duty,' DI Harris said after picking up almost immediately. 'But I'm pleased you rang. I expect you've got Gloria Van Haven's address.'

'Not yet, but I don't give up hope. I am at Lola's. In the manager's office. I tell you what I *do* have. Two men, each in possession of a handgun. I'm sure both guns were on that list circulated to all forces recently — the list of guns stolen from the RAOC depot in Scotland. I want to hand them over for your safe keeping ASAP.'

Harris needed no further instructions. 'Leave it to me. I'll have an armed unit there in no time.'

Angel closed the mobile, put it in his pocket and picked up the Beretta.

Suddenly there was a knock at the door.

Angel's heart raced.

The men on the floor stiffened, turned their heads and stared at the sound.

Angel looked down at them, stood up, waved the two guns and in a quiet voice said, 'Don't get excited. You're not going anywhere.'

Then he looked towards the door. 'Come in,' he called.

The door opened. It was another big ugly man. This one had fair hair.

Hans.

When Hans saw Angel standing facing him with a gun in each hand, he pulled the door shut and dived into the corridor, just before Angel had squeezed the trigger on the Walther.

The bullet landed in the door jamb.

Angel crossed the room to the door as fast as a tiger. He turned the key and locked it.

Out of his eye corner he saw Robertson surreptitiously edging away from Sebastian. He aimed the Walther and pulled the trigger.

Robertson's eyes jumped out of their sockets. 'Oh my God!' he screamed.

The bullet went through the cuff of his dinner jacket into the carpet a few centimetres from his head. His hands in the white linen gloves opened and closed several times.

'I said don't move. Keep perfectly still,' Angel said. 'Next time, my aim might be better.'

Then Angel positioned himself behind the door, held the Walther upwards and waited.

And waited.

Then he saw the door handle turn downward. Someone was trying the door. It was followed by a heavy banging.

'Open up,' a voice said. 'This is the police.'

Angel recognised DI Harris's voice.

He unlocked the door and six officers wearing bullet-proof helmets and body armour and carrying small repeater rifles streamed rapidly into the office, followed by a smiling DI Harris.

Angel sighed. Then assumed a satisfied smile and shook Harris's hand warmly.

Harris saw the two men on the floor. 'Are these the two for the paddy wagon?'

Angel nodded.

The police handcuffed Robertson and Sebastian and took them out.

Angel said, 'There should have been a third man called Hans. A lump of a man about twenty-five with fair hair. You didn't see anything of him on your way in, did you?'

'No,' Harris said.

Angel wrinkled his nose. 'These are their guns. The evidence that will put them away for five years each.'

He gave them to Harris, who bagged and labelled them.

Angel said, 'After the murder at the RAOC depot, we got that list I mentioned. Twenty-two guns, I think there were. There was definitely a Beretta Tomcat and several Walthers on that manifest.'

'I'm sure you're right,' Harris said.

Angel ran his hand through his hair. 'I want to get into that desk.'

Harris gestured towards it. 'Help yourself. I have an hour's work to do at the station, then I'm going back to bed for a while. I'll be up here later. You won't be here then, so I'll say thank you for the two customers and the hardware and be off.'

'You're welcome.'

'Goodnight.'

'Good *morning*,' Angel said with a grin.

Harris nodded, smiled and went out.

Angel was alone. He remembered the miniature recorder in his pocket needed switching off, then he busied himself going through each desk drawer systematically. He expected Robertson would have an address book.

Angel had looked thoroughly through the column of drawers on the right and the one in the middle. He started on the left column of drawers.

In the top drawer he found a half-empty box of .32 rounds, the right bore for the Beretta. He put the box in his pocket. DI Harris should have it. Being found in Robertson's desk was further evidence that the Beretta was in his possession.

Angel continued the search. He opened the second drawer down and there it was, a black-covered book with the word 'Addresses' embossed on it in white.

He caught his breath, then picked up the book. The first entry was 'Accountant' under A, with the name Oscar Starr next to it. Angel skipped through the pages to V and there it was, Gloria Van Haven's name, address and two telephone numbers. On the next page was an Alexander Velleman. It was an impressive address: *The White House, Whitehouse Road, Sheffield.*

At last. He pocketed the book, smiled and sighed with pleasure. He wondered if he could phone Gloria there and then. He had no idea of the time, but it had to be late. He checked his watch: 3.30 a.m. He was surprised. Phoning her was out of the question. He should be at home. In bed. Even if he left immediately, by the time he reached home and got between the sheets, it would be 6 a.m. Mary would be wondering where he was.

He walked through the empty nightclub, dark and quiet, to the front door. He screwed up his eyes in the street lights as he walked down the steps.

There were two uniformed policemen on the steps. They both said, 'Good morning, sir,' and saluted him.

'Good morning,' he said, and moved quickly along into the dark early-morning Manchester air.

Angel suddenly had a thought. He turned back. He went up to one of the constables. 'Excuse me, Constable. Are you in the same division as DI Harris?'

'Yes, sir. I am. "A" Division.'

Angel took out the box of the handgun rounds. 'Will you give him this box and pass on a message? I've just found these rounds in Robertson's desk. They're thirty-twos for the Beretta.'

'Certainly, sir.'

'Thank you, Constable. Good morning again.'

He stepped out into the dark.

It was cooler, fresher and smelled of kebabs, burnt cooking oil and chips. The constant hum of the motorway was interrupted only by the distant sounds of an ambulance siren and a barking dog.

Angel made his way the hundred metres to where he had parked the BMW. There was little traffic about. He crossed the street. A newspaper van raced past. As he approached the car, he pressed the remote and opened the car door.

Then the colossus Hans appeared silently from out of the dark and delivered a mighty blow from behind on Angel's neck, right on the track of his vagus nerve. He lost consciousness briefly and immediately sank to his knees, hanging onto the car door handle.

The blow was followed up by a mighty punch towards his chin. In his semi-conscious state, Angel pulled his head away and jerked the car door across in front of him. Hans's knuckles hit the door handle hard.

Hans gasped with pain and nursed his knuckles in his other hand.

Angel, now almost recovered, stood up and thumped Hans hard in the stomach. Hans leaned forward and Angel caught him with an uppercut to the chin.

Hans then reached inside his jacket and pulled out a gun.

Angel froze on the spot. Even in the dim light of the street lamp he could see that it was another old Walther PPK/S.

'Put up your hands, Angel,' Hans said. 'You're not getting out of this. Turn round and face the wall. One twitch and I'll pull this trigger.'

Angel had no option. With his hands in the air, he turned to stare at the stone wall of a house.

His heart sank. His mouth went dry.

His mind was all over the place. He closed his eyes in an attempt to stay calm. *Think, Angel, think.* Hans was definitely king in this situation, and any excuse or even no excuse at all would be enough for Hans to point that gun at his head and squeeze the trigger. And his life and his retirement with Mary would be history. He'd be in heaven . . . whatever that was like . . . separated from Mary . . . seeing his dear father again, maybe . . . or total darkness . . . nothingness . . . asleep without dreaming . . . never ever waking up.

He heard Hans speaking quietly on his mobile. 'I said I've got him. Would be easy enough to plug him. What does the boss want me to do? . . . Well, will you please ask him, Mr Starr?'

There was a long pause, then Hans's voice went up an octave and twice as loud. 'WHAT? . . . That's what the *boss* said? . . . Right, Mr Starr.'

It seemed to be the end of the call. Hans didn't say anything else.

Angel waited.

There was an uncanny silence behind him.

He waited. Waited for something to happen. Nothing did.

Then he moved his head slightly. 'Can I put my arms down now, Hans?'

There was no reply.

'Hans,' he called. 'Hans, are you there?'

Angel turned, to find that Hans had disappeared into the night.

SEVEN

30 Park Drive, Forest Hill Estate, Bromersley, South Yorkshire
Wednesday, 21 April, early morning

It was daylight on Wednesday morning when Angel arrived home.

Mary was awake but still in bed. When she heard the closing of the car door, she threw back the duvet, grabbed her dressing gown, and was putting it on as Angel came through the back door.

'What time do you call this?' she said.

He looked at his watch then swiftly grabbed her. 'It's time for a man to take his beautiful wife in his arms and give her a kiss.'

He pulled her towards him, put his arms round her and tried to kiss her, which was difficult because she was giggling. Eventually he succeeded.

Then he looked at the hall clock. 'It is ten minutes past eight, and I'm starving, dirty and tired.'

'I should think you are. I'll make you some tea and toast. Are you up for bacon and egg?'

'Ohhhh. Yes please, sweetheart,' he said as he began heading up the hall. 'But not for a few minutes. I'll have a shower first.'

'Right,' she called. 'I take it from this bright mood that you *found* whoever you were looking for.'

'No. But I have her address and phone number.'

The bathroom door closed.

An hour later, Angel was showered, fed and in bed asleep.

* * *

It was two o'clock in the afternoon before Angel woke up. He put on his dressing gown and shuffled into the kitchen, where Mary was preparing a small rack of lamb for their evening meal. He stood by the door and yawned.

She heard him and turned. 'Had a nice sleep?'

'Any chance of a cup of tea, sweetheart?'

'Of course,' she said and began to fill the kettle. 'Do you fancy something to eat?'

'Something quick,' he said. 'Have to go down to the office and then back to Manchester.'

Mary wasn't pleased. 'You're not going to be roaming round Manchester, and who knows where else, all night again tonight, are you?'

'No. Have I time for a quick shave?'

'Yes, of course. All these snack-type meals are wrecking my domestic arrangements, Michael. I need some streaky bacon, some milk and a drum of salt. Can you pick those up from somewhere? You'll forget, I expect. You usually do.'

'I'll remember.' Angel turned round to head for the bathroom. 'Don't you worry. Won't be long.'

At 3.20 p.m. Angel arrived at his office as bright and smart as a tin of white gloss. He found a piece of paper with a paperweight in the centre of it. He picked it up. It said, *Det. Sup. Harker wants to see you very urgently. Flora.*

He wrinkled his nose. He didn't look forward to that. He picked up his phone and tapped in a number.

It was promptly answered. 'Harker.'

'It's Angel here. You wanted to see me?'

Harker growled. 'Of course I want to see you. Come up here straight away.'

Angel recognised real anger in his boss's voice.

He promptly rushed up the corridor to Harker's office, knocked on the door and went in. It was the usual hot menthol fug.

Harker glared at him. 'Where the hell have you been? It's nearly half past three.'

Angel gave him a brief account of what had happened overnight in Manchester and explained why he had not surfaced until then.

Harker sniffed. 'You understand that the only reason you're *not* suspended is because you say this Gloria woman can provide you with an alibi.'

'Yes, sir. That's why I have to go back to Manchester today to see her.'

Harker sighed loudly. 'I've been giving you a lot of slack because of your father and because I detest anonymous letters, but I must be in possession of that evidence tomorrow at the latest. The chief constable is worried, as am I. We don't want a crank anonymous letter to cause me . . . the force, to treat you as a murder suspect.'

Angel didn't need his worries spelled out so explicitly. He was well aware of them.

He returned to his office. He tried to phone Gloria Van Haven on both numbers without success.

He set off in the BMW towards the M62. He drove over the Pennines and turned off one of the junctions onto a main road. On his left he saw a small supermarket and remembered the shopping. He drove into the car park and was in and out of the shop in no time, carrying a bag containing Mary's streaky bacon, milk and drum of salt, plus a pork pie. The last item was in case he felt hungry. He put it on the seat beside him, pleased that he had remembered.

He took the next right to another side road and arrived at Upper Shelldale. He soon found a modern block of ten or so flats in a pleasant-looking built-up area a few miles from

Manchester city centre. Gloria lived on the second floor, in flat number six. He soon found the door and pressed the doorbell. He heard it ring from where he stood. He waited. Nothing happened. He pressed the bell again. Still no reply.

A young woman carrying shopping was letting herself into the flat opposite.

They exchanged glances. Angel smiled politely.

'Are you wanting to see Gloria?' she said.

'Yes, but there's no reply,' Angel said.

'She'll not be in,' she said. 'She must be away. Haven't seen or heard her for a couple of days, actually. It's not like her. Can I take a parcel in for her . . . or anything?'

'No, thank you very much,' Angel said. 'I'll call back another time.'

She nodded, pulled her key out of her lock and went into her flat.

Angel, as soon as she was gone, immediately felt in his pocket for his wallet, took out his credit card, slipped it in the gap between the lock and the jamb of Gloria's flat and tapped it hard. Feeling it give, he turned the door handle, pushed the door open and walked in, closing the door quickly behind him.

The place was a tip. Every drawer was pulled open, with clothes hanging out, and cupboard doors had been left open. Clothes and sheet music were all over the floor. He checked the other rooms. Every one was the same.

Angel recognised the work of professional thieves.

Under the mess it was a very nice flat. The furniture was almost luxurious and everything was clean.

He meandered from one room to another, thoughtful. He wasn't sure what he was looking for. There was the diary or daily journal that Gloria had spoken of. That could be very valuable.

The average thief wouldn't be interested in that. He would want cash, gold, diamonds, jewellery, hard drugs, TV sets, bottles of whisky, brandy, gin, spirits . . .

There were a few plates, a cup and some cutlery in a bowl of water in the tiny kitchen sink, some dirty pots put to soak. The water was stone cold. If she was planning to go away, she wouldn't leave a few pots unwashed, would she? She might if she had rushed off in a hurry. He reckoned they had been there a couple of days at least.

Angel began the systematic search of each room. It took him two hours. It seemed to him that the thieves had done a good job. There was nothing there that was valuable or portable.

He had not found the journal, nor any bank or building society books, statements or paperwork.

He cleared some music and clothes off part of the settee and sat down. He simply didn't know what to do next. He needed to speak to the woman. He had to get that statement from her. He had exhausted most of the usual channels for finding somebody. He hadn't a single lead.

Unless she had been kidnapped too . . .

He looked at his watch.

He considered staying on in the flat for a few hours in case Gloria returned. Although, if she returned and found him in the flat the state it was in, she would naturally think that he was responsible. That would seriously jeopardise him getting a written statement from her. He would have to admit to her that he broke in like a common thief. He couldn't talk his way out of that.

If there was something he could do, here in Manchester, or anywhere for that matter, he would do it. But he had run out of ideas.

Tomorrow he would be suspended from duty, and he wouldn't have the status to find a way out of the outrageous accusation of murder.

Suddenly there was a noise outside, followed by a knocking on the door.

Angel stood up. He rushed to the door and stood with his back to the wall next to it.

At first he thought it was Gloria, but she wouldn't be knocking on the door of her own flat. Then he heard the rustle of paper through the letterbox, followed by a rectangular package in a large envelope dropping onto the carpet with a dull thud. Then there was silence.

It was the postman.

Angel picked up a couple of colourful leaflets from competing pizza restaurants and a large envelope containing something that felt like a book.

A book?

Angel sucked in a metre of air.

Instinctively, he knew it was Gloria Van Haven's journal.

She had posted it to herself to keep it safe. Clever girl.

He tore open the top of the fawn envelope and pulled out a red hardback book about twenty centimetres by fifteen. He opened it, and it began with the words, *Journal of Gloria Van Haven, Tuesday, January 1*.

He smiled and gave a deep, gratifying sigh.

He looked through a few pages at random and noticed that she didn't write an entry every day, but she never missed more than one or two days. He became increasingly interested, but he closed it determinedly and put it back in its envelope. He didn't want to consume time reading it where he was. He'd have plenty of opportunity for that later. Hopefully it would show he was totally innocent of the murder of Alfred Beecroft, as well naming some members of the Velleman gang. It might tie up some unsolved murder cases in the South Yorkshire area.

He put on his hat and, holding the envelope securely, quietly let himself out of the flat.

The corridor was deserted. He made his way past the stairs that led both up and down the building to the lift and pressed the call button. He heard the lift mechanism start up. It drummed quietly for a few seconds, then stopped and the doors opened.

To reveal Hans.

They caught each other's eyes.

Both men were momentarily frozen.

Hans suddenly stepped forward and said, 'I want you,' and he reached out for Angel's arm.

But Angel turned away and made a beeline for the stairs, bouncing down, taking three stairs at a time.

Angel could hear Hans's heavy breathing behind him. He reckoned he could outrun him.

He didn't want to lose Gloria's journal. He needed two fists to fight with, and he couldn't put the journal in his pocket.

Angel reached the ground floor, passed the lift, ran through the entrance and out into the street.

It was deserted. Nobody in sight. Nothing was moving.

He looked right, left and straight ahead, seeking an escape route. His car was only a few metres away, parked at the side of the road with a few others. He dug out his car key, pressed the remote and heard the click of the door unlocking. Then he saw Hans appear outside the flats. He looked around and saw Angel.

Angel darted to his car and managed to get into the driver's seat. He stuffed the journal under the bag of groceries on the passenger seat. He closed and locked the door just before the big man appeared at the window.

Hans tried the door handle. It wouldn't give. He pulled it violently. The car rocked. He continued yanking it. His lips curled back to show his teeth. His nostrils flared.

'Open up!' he bellowed. 'Open up!'

Angel ignored him, feverishly trying to get the key in the ignition. The engine started. At the same time the barrel of a gun smashed through the driver-side window. It touched Angel's head. It was cold steel. He froze.

Fragments of glass fell everywhere and three shards of shining glass stuck dangerously upward through the car door.

'Turn it off,' Hans said, his voice quivering with rage.

Angel reached down to the key in the ignition and turned it anti-clockwise. The engine stopped.

'Gimme the key,' Hans said.

What else are you going to do with an angry giant holding a gun at your head? Angel thought.

He passed him the key carefully. As Hans took it, he momentarily relaxed his other arm and lowered the gun away from Angel's head.

Angel took a chance.

He grabbed hold of the gun with both of his hands, pointed it away from himself and yanked Hans's arm further into the car and down onto a sharp and wicked-looking glass shard sticking up out of the car door.

'You bastard!' Hans shrieked.

A squirt of blood splashed and ran down on the outside of the car door.

The gun went off.

The noise was deafening in the confines of the BMW.

The bullet hit the fabric of the door opposite.

Angel kept up the pressure. The old Walther dropped into his lap.

Angel released his hold on Hans, who lifted his bleeding arm out of the window with his other hand. His jacket was soaked red, and blood was dripping onto the pavement. Hans held his arm outwards in considerable discomfort.

There was a low brick wall in front of a big garden, heavy with shrubbery.

Angel picked up the gun and pointed it at Hans. 'Back off and lean against that wall.'

Hans was content to do that.

Angel got out of the car, and pulling out his mobile called 999 and asked for a paramedic urgently. Then he scrolled down to DI Harris's number. The DI was not long in answering.

'I have another customer for you,' Angel said, 'and another gun.'

He explained about Hans's injury and told him that he had met him unexpectedly outside Gloria Van Haven's flat. He didn't mention that he had broken into her flat and taken the journal. He wasn't looking for any more trouble.

'I'll send a patrol car right away, and I'll be up there myself as soon as I can,' Harris said.

Angel slipped his mobile into his pocket, and without taking his eyes off Hans, he returned to his car and reached under the dashboard for a set of handcuffs.

A black Mercedes drove up to the door of Gloria's block of flats, stopped briefly, then drove away. Angel wondered who it was.

A blue-and-white paramedic's car arrived shortly afterwards. Angel waved it over.

The young man saw the gun Angel was holding. He blinked nervously.

'You'll have to put that away,' the paramedic said. 'I don't attend to patients when there are guns around.'

'This chap isn't your average patient. He is a gangster, a murderer. This is for *your* protection as well as mine.'

'I don't need your protection,' he said. 'The only distinction I make between people is whether they need help or not.'

'OK, OK. I'll keep the gun out of sight while you're working. But my finger will always be on the trigger, and I'll have no qualms about using it.'

The paramedic said nothing.

He looked at the wound. He took Hans's jacket off him, draped it on the wall, then with scissors he cut off the blood-soaked sleeve of the shirt above the elbow. He put it in a bag for disposal. He wiped Hans's arm and fingers with an antiseptic and applied a blue strap with a buckle as a tourniquet. He dressed the wound, wrapped it with bandages, then put the arm in a sling.

Then he said to Hans, 'Is that comfortable?'

'Yeah. It'll do, I s'pose.'

'How are you feeling? Are you feeling tired?'

'Yeah. A bit.'

The paramedic nodded knowingly.

Then he turned to Angel. 'He has to go to hospital immediately. He needs urgent treatment. He may possibly have to stay the night.'

Angel didn't like the sound of that. It provided too many opportunities for escape. Where was that police car?

'Well, I'm in your hands,' Angel said. 'Whatever's best.'

'I'll take him in my car,' the paramedic said. 'You can follow. It's only a mile down the road.'

Angel frowned. He didn't like that arrangement either.

The paramedic assisted Hans into his mini ambulance. Then he climbed into the driver's seat and pulled away.

Angel followed in the BMW, close behind.

He noticed in his mirror that the black Mercedes he'd seen was now following him. He didn't expect it to be friendly.

It was only a short distance.

Angel saw the big letters of the Manchester Grey General Hospital on the side of a building with many windows. He followed the paramedic to an area hatched out in yellow paint, marked 'FOR AMBULANCES ONLY', where the paramedic stopped. Angel pulled up close behind him.

The Mercedes had driven straight on and was out of sight.

Angel took a 'Police on call' card out of the glove compartment and placed it on the dashboard. Then he took the journal and the bag of groceries and put them in the boot, and locked it.

Hans was being sensible and was making no attempt to escape. He accompanied the paramedic up the slope and through a large door into the patient unloading area. Angel followed closely behind. The paramedic led them through another large door and down a corridor.

Several patients were being wheeled on trolleys through the door and down the corridor.

They followed the paramedic into an emergency treatment room, which was divided by curtains into cubicles. The man soon found one that was unoccupied.

As well as the usual hospital diagnostic and monitoring equipment, there was a bed and a chair.

The paramedic looked at Hans. 'Sit down. Are you all right? Not dizzy or tired?'

Hans sat in the chair. 'No.'

'Good,' the paramedic said and disappeared through the curtains.

Angel promptly took out his phone and rang DI Harris.

'We're at the hospital, Manchester Grey. The paramedic insisted. The patrol car didn't arrive at Upper Shelldale.'

'Sorry about that, Angel,' Harris said, 'but the roads are gridlocked with rush-hour traffic. I'm on the way. Should be with you in a few minutes. And I'll contact the patrol car and divert them.'

Angel thanked him and ended the call.

Then he took out the gun and waved it at Hans. 'Don't try any funny business. And don't think I won't shoot you if the occasion calls for it. All I need is an excuse.'

Hans glared back at him but said nothing. He was in too much pain to bother retaliating.

The paramedic returned.

Angel promptly put the gun back in his pocket but kept his hand round the grip.

'The doctor's coming to take a look,' the paramedic said, and he began unfastening the sling.

Angel noticed that the paramedic was now wearing skin-tight rubber gloves.

The unravelling of bandages began. A few minutes later an older man arrived, who Angel presumed was the doctor, and a conversation followed between Hans, the doctor and the paramedic.

A very short time after that, the cubicle curtain was opened a few centimetres. It was a nurse with DI Harris.

'Which of you is DI Angel?'

Angel smiled and stepped forward.

'Thank you, Nurse,' Harris said, crossing and standing next to Angel.

She rushed off.

Angel quietly explained the situation to DI Harris. 'When the doctor has finished with Hans, as this is your patch, I want you to take him into custody. Also, you should take possession of this old Walther; it's possibly another one of those stolen from the RAOC depot in Scotland. The only charge I have him on at the moment is possession of this firearm. There are others to follow.'

Harris nodded knowingly.

The nurse appeared through the curtain again. At her side was a police patrolman in all the protective gear and fitted radio communications. She looked at him and said to Harris, 'Is this who you are looking for?'

'Yes, Nurse. He's one of us. Thank you.'

The patrolman came into the cubicle grinning. The nurse closed the curtain and disappeared.

Angel said, 'This cubicle is getting overcrowded. I'll make one less.' He nodded a welcome to the patrolman and handed the Walther to Harris. 'It's loaded and the safety catch is off.'

He came out of the cubicle, glad to be relieved of that responsibility.

He retraced his steps, avoiding patients on stretchers being wheeled at speed by paramedics along the corridor.

He reached the hatched-out area marked for ambulances. He noticed it was powerfully lit and that the sky was turning to black. It was almost night. He looked at his watch. It was 6.30 p.m. He was more than an hour from home.

Mary will go mad, he thought.

Out of the corner of his eye he saw that damned Mercedes speeding away again.

Then he saw his own car. As he approached it, he became concerned.

He reached the BMW and his concern was justified.

The boot was open. He gasped. The bag of groceries had gone. More importantly, Gloria's journal had also gone.

His heart felt as if it was shrinking. His shoulders dropped. He sighed heavily. He stood for a moment, put a hand each side of his temples and said to himself, 'What the hell is it all about?'

He spent the next half-hour asking everybody who was in the vicinity if they had seen anyone near his car. Or if they had seen a black Mercedes.

Nobody had seen anything.

EIGHT

30 Park Drive, Forest Hill Estate, Bromersley, South Yorkshire
Wednesday, 21 April, 8.00 p.m.

Angel arrived home at eight o'clock feeling tired, weary, grubby and hungry.

'What time do you call this?' came the announcement from the kitchen.

What to tell Mary? He owed her the whole story, of course, but with certain details watered down or eliminated. He hated the distress and the anxiety that this was causing her.

He walked into the kitchen, steeling himself for another cross-examination.

Mary was wiping her hands on a tea towel.

'It's eight o'clock,' she said, hands on her hips. 'You're two and half hours late. And where's the shopping? You've forgotten it. It's too bad. I knew you would. The joint is dry. The meal is ruined. I can't depend on you for anything. You said you would be back in time and look at that clock.'

Angel looked at the ceiling and blew out a long breath.

'It's not fair,' she said. 'Why are you late? And what are we going to do without milk? If I had known, I could have gone out to the corner shop. It's too late as it is. What have you to say for yourself? Why don't you answer me? Are you listening? What excuse have got this time? It's gone eight o'clock. Well, what's your excuse? What's the matter? Cat got your tongue?'

Mary paused and looked at him closely.

He took a step towards her with his arms outstretched. 'Come here.'

She stepped up to him and they embraced.

'I've been out of my mind with worry,' she said tenderly. 'Why don't you get a proper job? There's still a shortage of teachers. They're enrolling them . . .'

Angel smiled. He'd heard it all before . . . many times . . . He gently stroked her back. 'I bought the milk, the salt and the bacon, you know, just as you wanted . . .'

'I didn't really think you would forget,' she whispered. 'Are they in the car?'

'They were stolen.'

'Stolen? What do you mean stolen?'

'While I was in this hospital,' he said.

Mary pulled away from him so that she could see his face. She looked surprised then concerned. 'What did you have to go to hospital for?'

Angel had got Mary thinking and therefore less angry. 'Now, I would like something to eat, sweetheart . . . I don't care what it is. I'm starving.'

'Why did you have to go to hospital. Were you hurt?'

'It's nothing for you to worry about. I'm perfectly all right. I'll tell you everything once I've had a bite to eat. A sit-down meal and time with you, Mary, is all I want right now.'

'You'll get your meal in five minutes, and like it or lump it,' Mary said. 'Correction. You may *not* like it. It'll be dry.'

Angel went into the bedroom, took off his jacket, shirt and vest, then dashed into the bathroom and washed his face, arms and hands. He put on a long-sleeved pullover, combed his hair, returned to the kitchen and sat down at the table.

Minutes later, Mary served up.

'Wouldn't your girlfriend give you the statement, then?' she said.

'I didn't see her. She wasn't there. And she isn't my *girlfriend*. I don't know where she is.'

Mary softened. 'What are you going to do?' she said.

He shook his head slightly several times. 'The best I can. I know Harker has no option.'

'Suspension *is* only temporary, though, isn't it?' she said.

'Suspension implies that I'm guilty of a crime, and I'm not. Also, suspension takes away my ability to make inquiries of my own. In fact, the force actually frowns on me making any inquiries at all. I am expected to be totally reliant on whoever they appoint.'

* * *

The next day was a day that Angel would never forget.

He arrived at the usual time — 8.28 a.m. — and took the BMW straight round to the back of the station. He soon found Sergeant Norman Mallin, who was the uniformed officer in charge of the maintenance and supply of station transport. He pointed out the missing window pane and the bullet lodged in the fabric of the door of the BMW.

'Those aren't big jobs, Michael. We can't take the lead out, but we can invisibly mend the fabric on the door. And if I've a window in stock, your car can be done today.'

'Thank you, Norman.'

He then went to his office and found a note on his desk. It was a formal letter from the superintendent, saying that Angel was to present himself at his office at 10 a.m. precisely.

He duly arrived as ordered.

Harker looked across his desk at him and frowned. 'I didn't want to have to do this, Angel, but I have no option. Wait there.'

Harker stood up and went out of his office to the chief constable's next door.

Angel looked round the office in the warm, menthol-laden atmosphere and wondered once again how Harker worked in such conditions.

After several minutes, he returned. 'The chief constable wants to see you.'

Angel followed Harker back to next door.

'Come in, Michael,' the chief said. 'Sorry that you find yourself in this predicament. I'm afraid that you are indeed suspended. You understand that I have no choice in the matter. However, you will be on full pay for three months, until the situation has been reviewed.'

Angel said, 'I hope it won't last anything like that long, sir.'

'Hopefully not. Now, regrettably, I have to ask you for your warrant card and badge.'

Angel's stomach quivered. He knew that this would happen, but it pained him more than he had expected.

He licked his lips. 'Yes, sir.'

He reached inside his jacket and passed the plastic wallet with his card and badge across the desk.

Then the chief constable said, 'I will be appointing a totally independent senior officer from another force to investigate this case, Michael. As soon as I have the arrangements confirmed, I will inform Horace . . . erm, Superintendent Harker.'

'Thank you, sir. It won't take long, will it?'

'It depends whether he can spare someone from his station who has the appropriate qualifications. But don't worry about that, Michael. I mustn't show any bias, but between the three of us, I expect them to find you, *and* this force, whiter than white in double quick time.'

Angel nodded, and was thinking how to reply when the chief constable spoke up again. 'There's something else, Michael.'

'What, sir?'

'It would stand you in very good stead if we did an unannounced search of your house — now, if you're agreeable.'

Angel pursed his lips and slowly blew out a lungful of air. 'Yes, sir. I've nothing to hide. But my wife might be somewhat alarmed if I wasn't there.'

The chief looked across at Harker. 'Organise that now, Horace. Take a team from the uniformed squad who are new, thorough and keen. You know Michael's wife, don't you? Break it to her gently, but not before you get there.'

'I will, sir,' Harker said. 'I'll get that organised immediately.'

The superintendent went out of the room and stood in the corridor.

The chief constable then turned to Angel. 'I want you to wait down here in your office until the search is completed, Michael.'

'Right, sir,' Angel said, and he followed Harker out of the office.

When the chief constable's door was closed, and they were walking down the corridor, Harker said, 'Now then, Angel, when this search is over, go home . . . relax . . . do some decorating . . . get some gardening done . . . have a day or two at Scarborough . . . enjoy yourself.'

Then he stopped and screwed up his eyes thoughtfully. 'Yes . . . you lucky devil . . . mmm . . . and you're getting paid for it. But always have your mobile switched on. I'll tell you if there's any need to come in.'

'Right, sir,' Angel said.

Harker went into his office.

Angel cursed under his breath. He shook his head. He had no intention of doing any of the things Harker had suggested. Absolutely none. He made his way down the green corridor to his own office. He sat down at his desk. He looked at the pile of post, reports and other paperwork needing his attention and pushed it to one side.

There was a knock at the door. It opened and DS Carter put her head through. 'Somebody told me you were back, sir,' she said.

'Come in, Flora.'

She closed the door. She was holding a newspaper. There was sadness in her eyes.

'Oh, sir. I am sorry to be the bearer of more, er, bad news . . .'

She broke off, brought up the newspaper and pointed to a glamour photograph spread over two columns. It showed a pretty young woman in a swimsuit with a banner draped diagonally across her, the words 'Miss Pennine Way' printed on it. She was holding up a silver cup. Above that was a headline: 'Ex Glamour Queen Shot Dead.'

Angel took it from her and read the text.

> *Gloria Van Haven, 46, celebrity, club singer, model, and past winner of Miss Pennine Way, was found dead in the River Irwell yesterday evening. Part of her body had been mutilated and she had been shot in the stomach . . .*

Angel's jaw dropped.

There was more about her early years, the hardships, the men in her life and so on. He read it then lowered the paper and looked at the wall. He couldn't believe what he was reading. Poor woman. He shook his head slightly. What was happening? She had been his only hope of providing an alibi for himself for the time the taxi driver was shot.

Carter could see Angel's reaction. 'Can I do anything, sir?' she said.

'No, Flora. Thank you,' he said, forcing a smile. 'You'd better be carrying on with whatever you have to do.'

She smiled reassuringly and went out.

Angel looked around the room. He had expected to be there for another twenty years or so. At that moment he thought that it could be the last time.

The phone rang.

He reached out for it. 'Angel.'

'Oh you *are* there, sir,' the familiar voice said. 'It's Don Taylor. I've got some strange results. Erm . . . relating to the Beecroft murder. Erm . . . is it convenient to come up?'

'Yes, Don. Of course.'

Angel put the phone down, his curiosity piqued.

A few moments later, there was a knock on the door and Taylor came in clutching a thin, light-brown paper file.

Angel looked up.

The SOC man looked worried.

'What's the matter, Don?' Angel said.

'The results from Forensics, sir. They've never been wrong, have they?'

Angel shook his head. 'We've been accepting their findings as absolute facts for . . . well, ever since I've had a warrant card. I've been to their laboratory. It's spotless. And the discipline and care they take with evidence is unbelievable . . . Anyway, what's the matter?'

From out of the file Taylor produced a sealed polythene bag containing a crumpled white handkerchief with a blue initial machine-embroidered diagonally across the corner.

'If you remember, sir, I found this handkerchief under the victim's body. Dr Mac was there and saw me bag it up. I thought the letter was "W", but actually I read it the wrong way up. It is, of course, "M".'

Angel pursed his lips thoughtfully. 'Yes, of course. I had some bought years ago. I've still got some. I'm still working my way through them.'

'And have they got "M" embroidered in the corner?'

'Yes, of course. "M" for Michael.'

Taylor inhaled deeply then sighed. 'According to the lab, your DNA is all over this handkerchief. And, in addition, I am sorry to say, sir, that from the vacuuming of the victim's chest, I extracted two hairs, each two centimetres long and complete with their roots, which are also confirmed to have your DNA.'

Angel looked up at Taylor's eyes. There was no frivolity in them. They were deadly serious.

Angel's heart felt like a lead weight.

* * *

Minutes later, from his open office door, Angel saw Harker and four uniformed constables leave the station to search his bungalow.

Angel shuffled back to his office and slumped down in the chair. He rubbed his chin and screwed up his eyes as he thought . . . The situation was serious. Some evil monster must have it in for him. The superintendent had enough evidence to charge him with Alfred Beecroft's murder . . . and there was nothing Angel could do about it.

He wished he was with Mary. He knew how confused and distressed she would be when the super and four young police officers arrived and showed her the warrant to search their home.

He dreaded the result of the search. He wouldn't be surprised if they found a ton of cocaine under the bed, ten million pounds in cash in the attic and the pantry wall made of 22-carat gold bullion bricks covered over with whitewash.

There was a knock on the door.

'Come in,' he called. He hoped it would be someone bringing him good news.

It was Norman Mallin. 'Your car is done, Michael. I've put it on your parking place. And here's the key,' he said as he put it on the desk.

'Thank you, Norman.'

Mallin went to leave then turned back. 'Good luck with . . . er, everything. I hope it works out all right.'

Angel knew his situation must be all round the station. He appreciated what Mallin was trying to say. 'Thanks, mate.'

Mallin gave him an encouraging smile and closed the door.

Angel felt a comfortable warmth from the man which was impossible to explain. It was a sort of peaceful encouragement.

There was another knock on the door.

It was DS Carter carrying several papers.

'Can I bother you again, sir?' she said.

Here was another who exuded comfortable warmth.

'You're no bother, Flora,' he said. 'Sit down.'

'I hear they're searching your house.'

He nodded. 'They'll probably find Shergar in the coal house.'

She smiled. 'I'm glad to see you're taking this so well.'

He shrugged.

'Nobody believes you murdered that taxi driver, you know,' she said.

'Thank you,' he said. 'But that won't keep me out of Armley jail.'

'Is there anything I can do, sir?'

'Thank you, Flora. Can't think of anything at the moment. No doubt there will be when I can think straight. What's that paperwork you keep waving about.'

She put it down in front of him. 'Maybe you want to deal with this while you're waiting?'

They were the documents relating to Sydney Fluke. He could see the young rascal's name at the top.

'Haven't we put that to bed yet?'

'I thought you'd like to advise me what to do . . . as a diversion from your own troubles?'

Angel clasped his hands and brought them up to his chin. 'This all started when he was accused of stealing a diamond ring.'

'Yes, sir,' Carter said. 'He was thoroughly searched but he didn't have it on him.'

'Since then he's committed three nuisance crimes.'

'Yes, sir. And every time he's brought in, he says he wants to make a statement and then changes his mind.'

'Now what would he want to make a statement about?'

Carter put her hand to her forehead. 'I can't think, sir.'

'Was it to do with *who* was there?'

There were a few moments of silence.

'Well, PC Weightman wasn't there on that occasion, sir. That's the only difference I can see.'

'Ian Weightman is one of the straightest men I know,' Angel said. 'And I've known him twenty-odd years. We were at school together. I don't think there could be anything dishonest about *him*. But I think we're on the right lines. There must be something . . .'

He breathed out and shook his head for a few seconds. 'I wonder if it has anything to do with the room that we were in?'

Suddenly, he jumped up and dashed out of his office and into the room next door, Interview Room 1.

Carter frowned but promptly followed him.

The room was as spartan as it could be. There were only four wooden chairs, a wooden table, a telephone and an audio recorder. When she arrived he had already upended one of the chairs and was scrutinizing the base and the cross member struts.

There was nothing.

He did the same with the other three chairs with the same result. He picked up the phone, turned it every which way it could be turned. Nothing.

He turned the table over and lowered it onto the carpet. He then got down on his knees, leaned across it and immediately saw in one corner of the framework of the table a light-brown wodge of dried chewing gum with a tiny curve of shiny platinum sticking out of it.

He felt a flutter in his stomach and licked his lips in anticipation.

He opened his penknife and edged the lump of hard chewing gum away from the wood, then stabbed the gum with his knife and picked it up to have a better look.

He smiled.

Carter gasped. 'Is that . . . ? It can't be, sir.'

'Yes,' Angel said getting to his feet. 'This is the diamond ring. Doubtless hidden here by Sydney Fluke. That's why he wanted to make a statement. He wanted to come into this particular interview room to retrieve the ring.'

Carter's face was clouded with confusion. 'Hidden,' she echoed. 'But, we searched him on the day . . . How the *hell* did he manage that?'

Then she brightened, flashing Angel a huge smile, her eyes dancing and shiny. 'That's great, sir. I don't know how you do it!'

'Couldn't have done it without your help, Flora.'

'I don't know about that, sir. What do you want me to do about wrapping it all up?'

'Say absolutely nothing to anybody about finding the ring, particularly Fluke. Find him and tell him that I want to see him. He'll want to come if he thinks he's a chance of getting into this room.'

'I'll get right onto it, sir,' Carter said with a smile and went out.

Angel put the table and chairs as they had been, and as he was returning to his office his mobile rang out. It was Mary.

'Hello sweetheart,' he said. 'Are you all right?'

'Don't you *sweetheart* me,' she said sharply. 'Why have you said it was all right to search this house without consulting me and why aren't you here? Why didn't you tell me?'

'I had no choice, Mary. It was on the order of the chief constable. I was there when he gave the order. They didn't find anything, did they?'

Mary's voice hardened. 'Oh no, Michael. Nothing much,' she said with a catch in her voice. 'They just went through our wheelie bins and found a linen bag from the building society and a black balaclava.'

Angel's mouth dropped open.

Mary said through her tears, 'Oh, Michael!'

NINE

Leeds Crown Court, Leeds
Friday, 23 April, afternoon

Friday, April 23 marked William Hart's first hearing in court. His face remained blank as the judge reeled off the list of charges against him. *Posing as a doctor, murdering two women, attempting to murder a third* . . . No one present expected him to make bail, and at the end of the hearing, he was sent back down to his cell to await transport to Breeming prison.

On the road from Leeds to Breeming prison, two miles from the A1, sat a railway crossing over a quiet B-road. It was on the main Kings Cross–Edinburgh route and was controlled by a signalman. The signal box stood in a corner position adjacent to both the railway track and the road.

Shortly after the judge had announced the sentence, two large men from the public gallery had left the court and driven away to Breeming crossing on a motorbike. It took forty-two minutes. They wheeled the bike through the pedestrian gate and parked it at the side of the track. They put their helmets and gloves on the seat, then went up the steps of the signal box. One of the men was carrying a new clothes line.

The signalman usually worked alone, but within a few seconds of the heavies' arrival he found he had unwelcome assistance. The heavies had donned clown masks while climbing to the signal box and, to add to the signalman's fear, were waving handguns around.

One of the heavies made a call on his mobile. 'Where is he?' he asked.

At the other end of the phone was the driver of an antique Rolls-Royce that had been parked at the rear entrance to Leeds Crown Court. The limousine was strategically positioned to be able to see and follow the special van carrying Hart to Breeming prison.

As the heavies and their signalman hostage waited, the driver of the Rolls gave frequent updates of the location of the van as he followed it two or three vehicles behind.

The heavies estimated the time of arrival of the van at the signal box, then tied up and gagged the signalman, closed the gates next to the track to road users, and finally positioned themselves on the pavement below to greet it.

The van duly arrived, and one of the heavies, still complete with mask, rushed to the cab and pointed his gun at the two men inside. 'Neither of you move.'

He assumed that there was an emergency button somewhere in the cab that had already been pressed, as soon as the hold-up and his presence were made clear. The button would have sent out a standard taped message to all receptive receivers on the police and prison wavelengths to the effect that an assault on the vehicle was taking place and urgent assistance was required.

The Rolls-Royce had now pulled up behind the van. The heavies knew that time was extremely short and they didn't waste a second. The plan had been well thought-out and rehearsed.

The driver opened the capacious boot of the Rolls and the heavies took a pair of long-handled heavy bolt cutters and jemmies out. They made quick work of the rear door hinges of the navy-blue prison van to reveal Hart and two other prisoners seated in small individual cages. There were about ten other cages lying empty.

Although they were wearing masks, Hart recognised his rescuers and his face burst into a smile, his eyes shining brightly.

'Thanks, chaps,' he said.

The other two prisoners took a keen interest in proceedings and looked hopeful.

The heavies cut through the bars round the lock with the bolt cutter. It took about three minutes working flat out. Then William Hart climbed out of the cage a free man.

'Come with me, Hart,' one of the heavies said.

The three men jumped down from the van to shouts of abuse from the other two prisoners.

Hart and one of the heavies ran along the pavement through the pedestrian gate at the crossing. They put on the helmets that were waiting for them on the seats of the motorbike. Then they mounted and drove away at speed on the path at the side of the railway track.

The other heavy and the driver entered the antique Rolls-Royce, the driver turning it around and driving slowly out of the quiet village of Breeming and into the countryside.

Forty seconds later, a police car arrived at the railway crossing. Over the following sixty seconds, two other police cars plus an unmarked car with three armed officers from Breeming prison arrived.

* * *

Angel was at home in the sitting room looking at a newspaper but taking nothing in. He had too much on his mind. He was trying to get used to the rules of his suspension — which forbade him from going anywhere near the station. It was a very strange sensation for him. He was expecting Horace Harker to arrive any minute and charge him with murder. It was a comfort for him to be with Mary. He could hear her in the kitchen, banging pots and pans about.

The house phone rang in the hall.

'I'll get it,' he called.

The noises from the kitchen stopped.

It was DS Carter calling from the station.

'I've got Sydney Fluke in reception, sir. Says he's got a message from you — that you wanted to see him and take a statement?'

Fluke. Angel gave a knowing smile. 'Can't you deal with this, Flora?'

'Yes, of course, but I thought you'd like to know.'

'Oh, yes,' he said. 'I'm glad you rang. You know what to do. You won't have any difficulty coaxing him into Interview Room 1 . . . not if I know Sydney Fluke. Let me know how you get on, eh?'

* * *

DS Carter went down the corridor through the security door to the reception area.

There was Fluke, leaning in the open doorway of the waiting room. He wore a frayed check shirt and blue jeans with holes in the knees. He had his hands in his pockets, and looked as though he hadn't shaved in days. As always, his jaw was slowly working on a large lump of chewing gum.

'Now then, Sydney,' Carter said. 'What can I do for you?'

Fluke blinked, frowned. 'Got a message to say Angel wanted to see me.'

'I've just spoken with DI Angel and he's far too busy to waste any more time on the likes of you.'

Fluke pursed his lips. His eyes narrowed. 'He's a funny copper, that one. Here I am. An accused man prepared to make a proper statement, and he doesn't want to know . . . ?'

'Look, Sydney. I have a few minutes before my next appointment. Don't let's shilly-shally about like this anymore,' she said. 'Let's do this right. Let's go into Interview Room 1. I'll set up the mic and you can say whatever it is you want to say.'

Fluke licked his lips, stuck his thumbs into his waistband and puffed out his chest. 'All right.'

DS Carter was pleased. She led the way back through to the interview room.

She opened the door and Fluke followed her in.

His eyes went straight to the table and the four chairs. He rushed to one of the chairs and sat down.

Carter deliberately turned her back on Fluke and busied herself with the recorder. She fumbled about, pretending to have difficulty getting it started.

She gave Fluke sufficient time to check two corners under the tabletop and find nothing. As she glanced back, she saw that he had moved to the opposite side of the table and was sitting there, his hands busy underneath it with a look of concentration on his face.

Carter was pleased. She didn't doubt that Fluke would soon find and retrieve the wodge of chewing gum he had hidden there on the last occasion he had been in that room.

She turned to him. 'Having some technical issues here, Sydney. Please bear with me while I run down the corridor to call in the techies. Won't be a minute.'

'*Awesome*,' Fluke said.

She went out into the corridor, turned right and opened the next door, which led to the gallery. She raced up a set of steps, opened a door and went into a tiny unlit room. A big window overlooking the interview room she had just left provided the light. There was only space for four chairs facing the big window. The nearest was occupied by Edward Scrivens, the eager young DC. She had arranged for him to be there to back her up.

He stood up when Carter came in. 'He's just found it, Sarge. Since you came out. He's behaving very strangely.'

'He's a strange one,' Carter said. 'What do you mean?'

'Well, he's taken out a small plastic bag . . . the sort bank cashiers use for silver and copper coins. He's put that dried-up wodge of chewing gum with the ring in it . . . look . . . now he's taking off his coat . . .'

Incredulous, Carter and Scrivens watched Fluke through the one-way glass. He fastened the little plastic bag to the top part of the inside of his coat sleeve, so that if he was patted down it would likely go unnoticed. He then put his coat back on.

'Come on, Ted. We've got all we need,' Carter said. 'You can search him. Find the ring. Then I'll arrest him and charge him. The inspector will be pleased. Finally some good news to cheer him up.'

* * *

30 Park Drive, Forest Hill Estate, Bromersley, South Yorkshire
Monday, 26 April, morning

Angel was at home feeling strange and unhappy not going into work.

After breakfast, Mary said, 'It's a lovely morning, Michael. And I think the lawn is ready for cutting.'

Angel looked out of the kitchen window at the garden still coming to life after the winter. The lawn was untidy, with small, dead branches from the trees and old, rotting orange and brown autumn leaves that had blown off onto the grass. He didn't want to do it, but it certainly needed attention, and it was a way of passing the time.

He went round the lawn with a black bin bag and cleared away the many small bits of branches and debris blown here and there by the winter winds. Then he humped the lawn-mower out onto the lawn, plugged it in through the kitchen window, and began cutting stripes up and down. He tried to enjoy the fresh air and the freedom of being outdoors, but his mind was on the forthcoming trial, which seemed inevitable.

He was halfway through a strip when Mary came outside and crossed the lawn to him. She was carrying the hand-set from the landline.

'Michael! You're wanted on the phone,' she said, handing it to him. 'It's the super.'

He took the phone, expecting bad news.

'Ah, Angel,' Harker said. 'The chief constable has appointed a man, Superintendent Piggott, who will be here shortly, to be the independent investigating officer commissioned to examine the case against you . . . and of course he'll want to ask you a lot of questions.'

'Right, sir,' Angel said, relieved but also a bit nervous.

'Well, put your best suit on, lad, and make a good impression.'

'I will, sir.'

'I don't know him, but the chief constable has a lot of faith in him. He'll be using your office while he's here. He should be here at nine o'clock.'

'I'll be there, sir.'

He switched off the phone and shoved it into Mary's hands. 'Thank you, love. I have to go in.'

He rushed inside and into the bedroom, undoing his shirt on the way.

* * *

At nine o'clock that morning, Angel was in what had until last week been his office, seated opposite Superintendent Piggott, who was sitting in what had been his chair.

Piggott was a tall man in his fifties. He had thick, heavy eyebrows and a big set of teeth which he enjoyed flashing occasionally, especially when he was smiling, which wasn't often.

On the desk in front of him was a thin file of papers, which he consulted from time to time.

'Now then, Angel,' Piggott began. 'I was sent this file of notes on the case collated by Detective Superintendent Harker . . . particularly, of course, recording your activities in connection with it. And I have spent the weekend putting them in some sequence and considering the evidence against you.

'I must tell you, Angel, I've defended some policemen in my time — most of them were innocent — but this one takes some beating. There is so much hard evidence against you that I really don't know what I can do for you. I'll do what I can, of course. But I think it only fair to warn you that you must prepare yourself for a long prison sentence.'

A shiver went down Angel's spine. He gave a very slight shake of the head and his lips tightened.

'I want to assure you, Superintendent,' Angel said, 'that I am entirely innocent of the murder of Alfred Beecroft and it seems to me that all the evidence has been deliberately planted.'

Piggott pursed his lips and sniffed. 'Well, we will have to see about that.' He looked down at his notes. 'Hmm. First of all, you have a clear motive.'

Angel said, 'That's not right, sir.'

Piggott frowned, giving his bushy eyebrows some exercise. 'It says here you were assisting a taxi driver, namely Alfred Beecroft, out of a parking problem and he ran over your foot, which required you to go to hospital.'

Angel nodded. 'That's true, sir, but—'

'Is it true Beecroft ran over your foot while you were assisting him?'

'At the time, I didn't know it was Beecroft.'

Piggott gazed at him then flicked his eyes upwards. 'Is it *true*, or is it *not* true, that Beecroft ran over your foot while you were assisting him?'

'Well . . . yes, it's true.'

'Good. Progress. And were you pleased about it?'

'No, sir.'

'Well then, you must have been *displeased* about it . . . to say the least. You must answer questions clearly and briefly, Angel, otherwise you may annoy the judge and confuse the jury.'

Angel sighed silently. He wasn't pleased, but he didn't want to annoy the man.

'Also, you appear to have no alibi. At the time of the murder, it says here, you were in the countryside only a few miles away from Beecroft's cottage. It says you were waiting for somebody who didn't show up. Is that correct?'

'Yes, sir.'

'Is there anybody who knew that you had this appointment?'

'No, sir.'

'Nobody?'

'No, sir. But as I have said before, it was rigged. I was set up.'

Piggott shook his head.

He looked down at his notes.

'And then, last Thursday, your chief constable quite rightly ordered your house to be searched without prior warning. The balaclava worn by the murderer and the white linen bag with the words "Bromersley Building Society" printed on it, used to carry the money which was taken in the robbery, were found in your wheelie bin. How do you account for that?'

Angel sighed. 'I can't, sir, only to say that the items were deliberately placed there to make me look guilty.'

Piggott shook his head slightly.

He looked down at the notes.

'Now, you say you found the victim but that you didn't touch him or anything else in his cottage.'

'That's correct, sir.'

'But *your* initialled handkerchief — you don't deny that it was *your* initialled handkerchief? — was found under the dead body of Alfred Beecroft.'

'I believe it could be mine, sir. But I have no idea how it got there.'

Piggott shook his head again.

Angel shuffled uncomfortably in the chair.

'It is *undeniably* yours, Angel,' Piggott shouted. 'There's no point in saying "I *believe* it could be mine." It *is* yours. It has your initial. It has your DNA.'

Angel blanched. 'All I am saying is that I don't know how it got there.'

Piggott looked back at his notes.

'We had intruders in our house shortly before this happened.'

'Did you report it?'

'Yes.'

'And what did they steal at the time?'

'We couldn't find that anything missing.'

'Why mention it now?'

'Because the intruder or intruders could have taken it at the time.'

'So your house was broken into to steal a used handkerchief . . . and nothing else?'

'Maybe a hairbrush . . . for the DNA.'

'There's no mention of a hairbrush here,' Piggott said, waving the sheets of the deposition about.

'I've only just thought of it.'

'And two hairs, again with your DNA, were found on the man's coat.'

He looked up at Angel.

'I don't know how they got there either.'

'It says here that when asked if you went inside the cottage, you said "No."'

'That's correct, sir.'

Piggott screwed up one side of his mouth and narrowed his eyes. 'Are you a doctor or something, Angel?' he said. 'If you stayed at the door, how could you know that Beecroft was dead from *that* distance?'

Angel wrinkled his nose, breathed in deeply. 'He had coagulated blood around his stomach. I could *see* that and I know old blood when I see it. And the top set of his dentures were half out of his mouth. If he had been breathing they would have fallen out. Also his eyes were open, looking upwards, and they did not blink for the full two minutes I watched him.'

Piggott sniffed. 'So, how do you explain the fact that two of your hairs were on the man's clothes and that your handkerchief was under his dead body?'

'I can't, sir. They must have been planted.'

Piggott ran his hand through his hair. 'What makes you say they must have been planted? If these intruders you refer to had you in their sights, you would have been dead too by now, surely.'

Angel's bottom lip curled back across his teeth. 'If I had been shot dead it would have been a three-day wonder. But it would be a feather in the cap of a gang leader to see me, one of their biggest enemies, in prison. Think of the prestige he would earn in the underworld. *Copper gets life for murder.* I would be ridiculed and disgraced for the rest of my life, while he would be seen as a genius.'

Piggott sighed.

Angel felt a quiver in his stomach.

TEN

30 Park Drive, Forest Hill Estate, Bromersley, South Yorkshire
Monday, 26 April, late morning

'How did you get on, love?' Mary said.

Angel slumped down in the chair. 'I don't think he believed a word I said.' He rubbed his chin.

'I'm sure he did. You have an open, honest face.'

'Huh. There's such a weight of evidence against me, some circumstantial, and some laid by Velleman's gang.'

'What are you going to do now?' she said.

He rubbed his chin.

'I don't honestly know. I've got to get that journal back . . . somehow.'

Mary looked at him fondly. 'I wish I could help.'

'You do. *Every day*, by simply being here and listening,' he said, then he stood up. 'I'm going for a walk.' He rushed out to the hall.

'Oh. Don't be long. Have lunch before you go.'

'No,' he said, grabbing his hat from a peg in the hall. 'Be about an hour.' The front door slammed.

Mary knew why he had gone for a walk. He needed to do some heavy thinking. When he was among the trees and bushes of the park he could amble and think without interruption.

* * *

It was early that afternoon that Angel pulled his car up outside the block of flats in Upper Shelldale.

He went in the lift up to the second floor and went round to flat number eight, the flat opposite Gloria Van Haven's flat.

As he looked at the door, he felt in his top pocket for his miniature recorder. He switched it on and turned the recording level to 'high'.

Then he put his finger on the bell and pressed.

The door opened and a pretty face looked at him over a short chain.

Angel put on his best smile. 'Remember me? My name is DI Angel. I came to see Gloria last Wednesday, but she wasn't in.'

She relaxed. 'Oh, yes, I remember. I never would have guessed you're a policeman. But I've told all I know to the police already.'

'There are just some details I need to clear up . . . if you could spare the time.'

'Just a second,' she said. Then she closed the door, unfastened the chain, stood back and pulled the door open wide.

With an open hand gesture she pointed to an upholstered chair by the imitation coal fire, and she sat opposite him on a settee. Angel noted her wedding ring.

'It was so sad to read about her death,' she said.

Angel nodded. 'Did you know her well, Mrs . . . erm . . . ?'

'Pascal,' she said helpfully.

Angel smiled, trying to look confident. He no longer had his warrant card and badge. If she had asked for proof he was from the police, he would have been in difficulty.

She inhaled deeply. 'No disrespect, Inspector Angel, but I've already told at least two different policemen all I know about Gloria.'

Angel nodded, 'So you have, Mrs Pascal. But I don't just want facts I can put down on a form to be filed away. What I really want is to catch her murderer. I *do* want that. It was a savage, evil killing made much worse by dumping Miss Van Haven in that dirty, cold river. Every decent person wants to catch the murderer so that they're punished, but also so they can't do it to some other poor woman, don't they? Don't you?'

Mrs Pascal breathed more quickly. 'I certainly do,' she said.

'Whatever you can tell me about the people who visited Gloria over the last three months or so may possibly help me. I need leads to be able to build up her lifestyle, which hopefully will steer me towards finding her murderer.'

'Well, Inspector, she told me that she had to keep her address private or she wouldn't get a moment's peace. She said that many of the wrong sort of men who saw her around, well dressed and in a big expensive car, got the wrong idea about her. They thought she was rich. They also thought she was on the game or desperate for a man. And she was neither. She had a man who frequently visited her and stayed the night, Inspector. I know because I often saw him arrive and sometimes leave. A chauffeur used to drive his old Rolls-Royce up here at any old time, drop him off with an overnight bag, and then drive away quickly.'

'Did you get to see the man?'

'Oh, yes. Only from a distance though. Through the window. He was a tall man, distinguished-looking. A bit of extra weight on him. Always wore a smart suit. He didn't hang about. He used to rush out of the car to the front door.'

'What was his name?'

'I don't know. Gloria never said. I never asked. She was always very secretive about him. It was as if he never existed.'

Angel rubbed his chin. 'And how often did he call?'

'Once or twice a week, I think. That was until about a month ago, when his visits dropped off.'

Angel listened to her intently.

'I knew when he *wasn't* visiting,' she said. 'Gloria would pop across to me, and I'd see her going out to the shops and having her hair done. When he *was* there, I never saw her. She only left the flat at around quarter to eight at night to go to work at Lola's nightclub.'

'Thank you, Mrs Pascal, that's most helpful. Now, was there anybody else?'

'No. Not that I was aware of,' she said.

Angel stood up. 'Thank you, Mrs Pascal. I must be off.'

She looked down at her manicured hands, fiddled with her wedding ring, then coughed to clear her throat. 'I'm in a quandary, Inspector.'

He pursed his lips and resumed his seat. 'Anything I can do to help?'

'Gloria told me something and made me promise not to tell anybody under any circumstances.'

'Of course, I have no idea what it is, but don't you think trying to find the identity of her killer overrides any promise you made her, now that she's dead?'

'I don't think what she told me has any bearing on her murder, Inspector.'

'Don't you think I should be the judge of that?'

She tilted her head slightly, sat motionless for a few seconds, then said, 'Very well, but promise me you won't use the information unless it is absolutely necessary.'

'You can rely on me, Mrs Pascal,' he said.

She exhaled then looked into Angel's face and began. 'Gloria had a lover. His name is Brian Fellowes. He's a really handsome man. I've met him and he's charming. He owns Fellowes Fairs. You'll see his vehicles going to fairs all over the place, round here and over in Yorkshire. You're bound to have seen them on the roads. Big diesel trucks towing a caravan, sometimes a trailer. But look, Brian is married. And wishes he wasn't. He's very well off. But if his wife finds grounds for a divorce and wins, she'll get half his business. Gloria said he owes a lot of money to the bank, and he wouldn't be able to pay them, so he'd have to sell some of his rides. That would break his heart. He loves those machines, they're proper old Victorian ones. Lovely decorations, painted ladies, pirate galleons and all kinds of animals. They're impossible to replace. You see why it needs to be secret about him and Gloria?'

Angel nodded. 'Indeed I do. You can rely on me. If Mr Fellowes is innocent of a crime, his name will be kept out of this enquiry.'

'Thank you, Inspector.'

Angel stood up. 'I must go. You've been most helpful, Mrs Pascal.'

She smiled and led him to the door.

Then Angel, in a most casual way, said, 'Oh, did you know Gloria kept a journal?'

'Oh yes. She called it her "insurance policy". I never quite knew what she meant.'

Angel knew exactly what Gloria had meant.

'Do you know where it is now?' he said as he made his way out.

'No idea.'

'Thank you very much, Mrs Pascal.'

The door closed.

Angel reached into his pocket and switched off the recorder.

* * *

The following morning, Angel turned the BMW off the main road between Oldham and Bromersley onto a field in the middle of a village behind a row of shops.

Angel saw several large diesel vehicles with the words 'Fellowes Fairs' painted on the cab doors. There were fifteen or more trailers covered with tarpaulins and another dozen or so caravans.

He stopped the BMW on the edge of the field, not wanting to get stuck in the mud. He looked out through the windscreen and saw six grubby-looking men — of various ages, mostly in trousers and oily vests —assembling the foundation of a large circular ride. He finally got out of the car and walked across the field to an old woman hanging washing on a line between two caravans.

'Excuse me, madam,' he said. 'Where would I find Mr Brian Fellowes?'

'He's in yon office,' she said, pointing to a particularly smart four-wheeled trailer behind a well-polished black Mercedes saloon.

'That's his car, so he'll be in there,' she added.

Angel thought he recognised the car. It was the Mercedes hanging around Gloria Van Haven's block of flats the night he had been attacked by Hans. It had subsequently followed him to the hospital, where the journal had been stolen from his boot — not to mention Mary's groceries.

He thought an interview with Mr Fellowes should be quite promising.

As Angel approached the trailer he saw the word 'Office' written on the door. He reached up to his pocket and switched on the tiny recorder, then knocked.

A man's face appeared at a window. The window opened and he said, 'Hello? Yes? Can I help you?'

'My name is Detective Inspector Angel. I'm looking for Brian Fellowes.'

'That's me. Police? Did you want to see my licence?' he said. 'You should know me by now.'

'No. It's nothing to do with a licence, Mr Fellowes. I need to see you *alone*.'

The smile left Fellowes' face and his eyes narrowed.

'You'd better come in,' he said.

Angel pulled himself up the three steep steps into the office on wheels. He carefully noted the sort of lock on the door handle for later.

He went inside. It was equipped with all the usual needs of a small, modern office.

'Now, Inspector Angel. What's all this about? Whatever do you want to speak to me about — alone?'

'It's about Gloria Van Haven.'

He blinked. 'I don't think I know her.'

Angel smiled knowingly. 'Whoa there! Let's be careful what we say, Mr Fellowes. You wouldn't want tell me a deliberate lie, would you?'

'I remember the name . . . vaguely . . . I think.'

'Hmm. Well, "vaguely" is an improvement on "I don't think I know her." Can you improve it a little more? "Yes, I knew her very well," perhaps?'

Fellowes suddenly changed tack. 'What is this all about, Angel?'

'Are we going to talk sense, Mr Fellowes?' Angel said. He took his tongue out of his cheek. 'I'm trying to find Gloria Van Haven's murderer. So I'm talking to anybody who knew her . . . anybody who might have had a motive.'

'Oh. Well, I hadn't a motive. I loved her, Inspector. I miss her. That lets me out, doesn't it?'

'Maybe. But do you know anybody who did have a motive? Did she ever say she was afraid of anybody?'

Fellowes didn't answer. He just sat there thinking, turning his head a little to the right for a few seconds . . . then a little to the left . . .

'If you know anything, Mr Fellowes,' Angel said, 'it is your moral duty to tell me.'

After several more seconds Fellowes said, 'There is a man . . . James Robertson. He's the manager of Lola's nightclub, where she worked. She was terrified of him. She found out that he'd murdered a taxi driver, and he threatened to kill her if ever she told anybody. It was something to do with a robbery, and they were trying to set up a cop too.'

Angel was naturally elated at that information, and that it would be recorded on his pocket recorder.

‘Did you get that from her journal?’ he said.

‘Yes. It’s there in black and white,’ Fellowes said.

‘Have you still got the journal? You know, the one you nicked from my car the other day . . .’

Fellowes hesitated before replying.

‘No,’ he said.

Angel wasn’t happy. ‘I feel I should warn you, Mr Fellowes, *that* journal is a significant silent witness in this murder inquiry, and it would be a serious offence to withhold it from the police.’

‘I haven’t got it and I have no idea where it is,’ Fellowes said.

Angel frowned.

Fellowes put his hand to his chin and squeezed his lower lip thoughtfully. ‘I may have said too much already, Inspector. You don’t know these people. I’ve probably just signed my own death warrant.’

‘Not at all,’ Angel said. ‘I don’t have to say where I get my information from.’

‘They have spies all over the place.’

Angel thought he had all the information Fellowes was willing to give, so he took his leave, returned to his car and drove off site, back onto the main road.

He made for home.

When he had turned onto the familiar road leading to Bromersley, he got to thinking. He couldn’t be absolutely certain about Fellowes. He was obviously afraid of Velleman’s gang . . . seriously afraid, and that wasn’t surprising, with all their muscle and the personal armoury they possessed.

Fellowes might see the journal as a two-edged sword. Velleman would want Fellowes’ blood if he got hold of it and read that Gloria was having an affair with Fellowes. *That* could very well sign Fellowes’ death warrant. However, if Angel could get the journal back, there was enough evidence in it to bring charges against Velleman and the others in the gang, leaving Fellowes free from their unwelcome attention.

Something else occurred to Angel. If Fellowes had Gloria’s journal, he surely would not keep it at home to risk his wife finding it. He would have to keep it in his car, or his mobile office.

He wondered how much of his new findings he should share with Piggott.

* * *

It was seven o'clock that evening when Angel returned to Fellowes' fair. He parked the BMW on the main road in a good position to observe vehicles leaving the field.

He got out of the BMW and mingled with the thin stream of customers as they entered the field and shambled up to the fair.

The raucous music and flashing coloured lights beckoned customers to the rides and the side stalls.

The haphazard way he thought the fair vehicles had been parked earlier that day now made sense, and the brightly illuminated rides and stalls were positioned together like a jigsaw puzzle. The diesel generators, trailers, live-in caravans and other ancillary vehicles formed a U shape around them.

He found the black Mercedes still parked outside the mobile office, and he saw the silhouette of Brian Fellowes' head and shoulders lit up against a window of the office. He appeared to be still working at his desk.

Angel ambled out of the fair and returned to his car.

He settled himself in a comfortable position, where he would be able to see the Mercedes come out of the field and onto the main road.

He expected a long wait, and it was about nine o'clock when he finally saw Fellowes pull out of the entrance to the field, look right, look left and look right again. Then he was gone.

Angel got out of his car and opened the boot. He took out two heavy pieces of steel tubing about half a metre long, with slightly different diameters, so that one fitted inside the other. He discreetly dropped them down inside his trousers. They each had a wire hook at one end to hang over the trouser waistband. He patted his jacket to check that he had his small but powerful torch there. Then he locked the BMW and made his way to the fair.

Crowds of adults and children had gathered around the rides. There were queues everywhere. The sideshows were also taking money. The music was louder and the lights on the rides and stalls seemed brighter. The diesel engines were noisily grinding out power and it seemed that all the fairground employees, and their children, were busy taking money.

Angel ambled his way to Fellowes' office. He watched it for a couple of minutes to see whether there was anybody around. Satisfied that there wasn't, he tried the handle of the door. As he expected, it was locked.

Then he took the tubes from down his leg. He put the bigger tube over the handle, then pressed the other end of the tube downward. Nothing happened. Then he slipped the smaller tube down into the bigger tube part way so that the overall length of the handle was about a metre long, giving him more purchase, then he applied his weight to that. The sheer force snapped the metal and the door opened.

Angel felt a flutter of relief in his stomach and he breathed out a long sigh. He put the tubes together and took them into Fellowes' office with him.

He could still hear the music, and there was some light from the glittering machines and lights of the fairground. He was thankful for that. It allowed him to use the tiny torch sparingly.

There was a filing cabinet. He looked through that. There was a desk. He looked through that. There was a computer desk. He looked through that. And he looked through the stationery cupboard. The journal wasn't there.

He tilted his head down and frowned.

Then he wiped his prints methodically from the drawer handles, cupboard doors and so on. After that, he stood in the middle of the office, thumbing his ear, thinking that he must have been wrong, when he spotted several account books and files on top of the filing cabinet. He shone the torch on them. The bottom book was the right size. In the unnatural light the colour was indistinct. He pulled it out, opened it up and read the top line. *Journal of Gloria Van Haven. Tuesday, January 1.*

Bingo!

He breathed out quickly, and found himself grinning uncontrollably.

His only thought now was to get home to Mary.

He put the journal under his coat and squeezed it with his arm. He picked up the steel tubes, peered through the window to see if anybody was around, then opened the door and went down the three steep steps backwards, holding onto one of the hand rails.

He heard a rustle of clothing behind him. As he turned, somebody banged the back of his head with a metal bar the size of Blackpool Tower and he collapsed like a blancmange.

* * *

In his sleep, he felt something sharp biting his arm. He tried to pull away but he was being held down . . . then he was floating on a cloud . . . he wanted to sleep . . . someone was pushing him out of a car . . . he had to stand up . . . it was a struggle . . . a car horn sounded . . . then another . . . vehicles whizzed passed both in front and behind . . . he wanted to sleep . . . a car was being driven straight at him . . . it stopped with a squeal of the brakes . . . he leaned on the bonnet to help him to stand . . . the driver yelled at him . . . again car horns were being sounded all round him . . . he wanted to sleep again . . . another came at him at speed . . . it stopped and the horn sounded, and he heard an angry voice say . . . 'drunken slob' . . . and another angry voice said . . . 'get off the frigging motorway' . . . a big car stopped and a man with shiny silver buttons on his coat pushed him brusquely into the back of it . . . he welcomed the chance to sleep, but the man asked a lot of questions . . . Angel didn't know anything

. . . he slept a while, then he was shaken by Silver Buttons with a mug of coffee . . . he enjoyed it.

He finally woke up properly, and looked around. He suddenly realised he was in a cell. He was in a police station. And it wasn't Bromersley. The atmosphere was the same . . . the rattle of handcuffs and keys, the sound of phones ringing and the smell of chalk and paper.

He remembered that he had found Gloria's journal. But where was it?

As he sat up on the bunk bed, he looked around. He felt an irritation on his left arm. He pulled up his coat sleeve and saw a purple-and-red patch on his skin. He rested back on the hard pillow and found a lump on the side of his head.

There was a sudden rattle of keys and the cell door opened. A young PC carrying a clipboard and pen came in. 'Now then, have we sobered up enough for a few questions?' he said chirpily.

Angel struggled to sit up on one elbow. 'Yes, lad. And my first question is, did I come in here with a book?'

'No. You came in as you are, except that you were drunk.'

The journal had gone . . .

'I wasn't drunk,' Angel said, then uttered a long sigh and closed his eyes.

The constable peppered him with questions, which he waved away. He was too tired and distraught to say anything more.

The constable gave up after a few minutes.

Angel fell into a deep sleep.

After a while, he was awoken by a man sitting on his bunk. He had a stethoscope round his neck and he was holding his wrist.

Angel looked at him bleary eyed. 'What's happening?'

'Checking your pulse,' the man said. 'I'm a doctor.'

After moment or two, he removed his hand. 'That's all right.' Then he pushed up Angel's sleeve and looked at the purple-and-red mark. 'What's this?'

Angel rubbed his eyes and murmured, 'I dunno.'

'They said that you insisted that you weren't drunk, and if you're telling the truth, then it seems you were injected with something which seemed to have that effect.'

Angel nodded.

'Well, you certainly don't smell of alcohol. What did they give you?'

'I dunno.'

The doctor took a blood sample from Angel's other arm. Then he packed his bag and exited the cell into the station's reception.

Angel felt his eyes shut once more. He slept the sleep of the dead.

When he woke, it was 6 a.m. on Wednesday. He felt more human. The cobwebs and out-of-focus veils around his eyes had cleared. His vision was perfectly clear again. His head still throbbed, and he found a painful bump at the back of his head. He eased himself up off the bunk, looked through the bars at the green painted wall and called, 'Anybody there?'

No response.

He tried again, louder. 'Anybody there?'

Somewhere out of sight, a door opened. A big man in a sergeant's uniform appeared. He walked down the short corridor and through the open door of the cell. He looked down at Angel and smiled.

'And how are we now?' he said.

'I'm fine,' Angel licked his dry lips. 'Any tea going, Sergeant?'

'There will be soon, sir. By the way, we've had your identity confirmed by Superintendent Harker at Bromersley. Also, the doc's bloodwork confirms you were sober, but you were injected with something nasty. Now we just need to find out what. So when you're fit, you're free to go.'

Angel nodded. He thought a moment. 'Where am I?'

'A small nick called Upper Barrow, on the main road between Oldham and Bromersley. One of our patrols brought you in from the M1.'

‘When I arrived here, did I have a book on me — a sort of diary?’

‘You had nothing, sir.’

Angel wrinkled his nose at this.

The tea materialised and he sipped at it eagerly. He was even persuaded to have some toast.

Then the sergeant drove him back to the fairground. But whatever evidence he was expecting to find there was long gone. The fairground workers had already packed up and moved on. There was not a vehicle in sight. A trail of lager cans, crisp packets and other detritus was the only sign that they’d ever been there at all.

The sergeant then drove Angel to his car. Angel thanked him for his care and attention and promptly made for home.

ELEVEN

30 Park Drive, Forest Hill Estate, Bromersley, South Yorkshire
Tuesday, 27 April, 8.00 a.m.

Angel arrived home at around eight o'clock that morning.

Mary wasn't in the kitchen. He peeped into the bedroom. The curtains were closed, but he could see she was still asleep. He smiled. He put the kettle on, made two mugs of tea, and took them into the bedroom. He drew back the curtains.

Mary opened her eyes.

She pushed a handful of her fair hair out of her eyes, sat up and looked across at Angel. 'Oh, Michael. What time is it? You should have woken me. How long have you been back? I'll get up and get you some breakfast.'

He sat on the edge of the bed and pointed to the mug on the bedside table. 'There's no rush, sweetheart.'

She reached out for it. 'Oh thank you, darling.' She took a sip then looked at him closely. 'You didn't get the journal?'

'No,' he said, looking down at the carpet.

He gave her a much-edited run down of what had happened and finished up saying, 'Now I want a quick shower and some clean clothes. I'm going to Leeds.'

'And I must get up,' Mary said, and whisked back the duvet.

* * *

Armley Prison, Leeds
Tuesday, 27 April, 10.30 a.m.

Angel parked his car in Armley Prison car park and walked the rest of the way to the main entrance. The outer door was open, so he went to the inquiry window.

'Anybody home?' Angel said.

A stern old face appeared. 'What do you want?' the prison officer said. 'Oh, it's you, Michael.' His miserable expression changed to a warm smile. 'How are you going on?'

'Hello, George,' Angel said. 'Oh, personally, I'm fine. But I keep sending them to you to serve a ten-*year* sentence. You keep them for ten *days* and then let them go free.'

His friend chuckled. 'It's the law, Michael. It's the law. There hasn't been an escaped prisoner from here for years, and we intend to keep it that way. If we let them out, it's because we've been so directed by the court. You know that.'

They both grinned, then the prison officer looked down at his book. 'Now, what can I do for you, Michael? Oh yes, I see that you have permission from the governor to see a prisoner. I'll take you up myself.'

He escorted Angel through the processes of admission, including being patted down for weapons, and was finally delivered to a little interview room.

Angel thanked him and George took his leave.

The room was sparsely furnished with a table and two chairs. Angel took the chair opposite the door and sat down. He was aware that he could be observed from hidden cameras, so he would have to do what he wanted to do surreptitiously.

He took his handkerchief from his trouser pocket, coughed into it, wiped his lips, then put it back into his top pocket. At the same time as he tucked it in he switched on his tiny recording machine.

A few minutes later, the door opened and Sam Spinetti came in, followed by a prison officer.

Angel wasn't at all surprised to see him there, but Spinetti's eyes opened wide when he recognised Angel.

At first the pickpocket seemed pleased to see the policeman, then he became apprehensive.

A jerk of the head from the prison officer in the direction of the chair was sufficient instruction for Spinetti to sit there.

The prison officer went out, closed the door and locked it.

Angel took a pack of cigarettes out of his pocket, which he had bought on the way to the prison, and put it on the table in front of him.

Spinetti's eyes locked onto them like a searchlight on a heavy bomber.

'Ooooh,' he said, and licked his lips. He reached out for the cigarettes.

Angel beat him to it and snatched the packet up, holding it firmly but keeping it on show.

A few moments later, he smiled. 'The last time I saw you, Sam, you told me that Gloria Van Haven had had a relationship with William Hart. You said they lived together. You also said that he had left her. I wondered if you had picked up anything else.'

Spinetti leaned forward toward Angel and in a low voice said, 'No, Inspector, nothing. I hope you didn't tell anybody that I told you.'

'Of course I didn't,' Angel said.

'Do I get the ciggies now, Inspector?'

'Never mind the ciggies. What can you tell me about Alexander Velleman?'

At the mention of the name, Spinetti blinked uncontrollably for several seconds and his hands trembled. Continuing in a low voice, Spinetti said, 'Nothing, Inspector. I told you all I know.'

'What do you know about Oscar Starr?'

Spinetti's jaw trembled. 'N-n-nothing.'

'I think you do.'

'Only that he's one of *them*.'

'Okay,' snarled Angel, 'let's get back to Ms Van Haven and her tangled love life. Surely there's more you can tell me about that.'

'I know that between others she had a fling or two with a married man called Fellowes,' Spinetti said. 'He runs a big fairground business. But after Gloria died, his rich wife found out everything. The last I heard she was threatening to leave him — I don't know anything more, Inspector. Honestly.'

There was a pause. Angel looked straight at him. 'I believe you do,' he said.

'Oh no, sir,' Spinetti protested.

'Which one of Velleman's gang paid you to hide my mobile?'

'It wasn't me. I never touched your mobile.'

'Come off it, Sam. You're the best dipper in the business. I don't know of another dipper who could have taken it out of my pocket as perfectly smoothly as you did . . . not for miles around.'

Spinetti relaxed on hearing such a compliment, even if it was from a Police Inspector. He smiled. 'I didn't t'ink as how you had noticed,' he said.

'I didn't. I worked it out after I found it under my desk when I returned to the nick. You were the only one it could have been.'

'To tell the truth, Inspector, I dared not refuse,' said Spinetti. 'I thought it was a sort of prank, honestly. Just hiding your mobile. I didn't t'ink as how it would do you any *real* harm. Just an inconvenience. That's all.'

'Who set you up?'

Spinetti pulled a weary face. 'I can't remember.'

Angel sighed. 'If you can't remember now,' he said, 'you'd better remember when you're in the witness box in court.'

Spinetti's jaw dropped. He felt hairs rise along his arms.

'If I told you *that*, Inspector, my life wouldn't be worth a Waterford sprat.'

Angel sighed. 'How much would it be worth if you had to tell it in court for the world to hear?'

Spinetti's bottom lip quivered. 'You're very cruel to me, Inspector Angel,' he whined. 'Very cruel.'

'The world is a cruel place, Sam. Don't you realise that your *friends* who you are so quick to *protect* have set me up for murder, a serving police officer?'

'They're no friends of mine, Inspector,' Spinetti said. 'If they found out I had said anything to you, they would have cut my gizzard, filled me wit' lead and thrown me in the river in no time.'

Angel put the pack of cigarettes very deliberately on the table.

Spinetti sighed then he said, 'Well, may God help me when my time comes. I was just coming out of Rotherham market about three weeks ago, when my mobile rang. It was James Robertson. I didn't know him well, but I knew what a bully he was. He said they had a laugh on wid you and he said that he needed you to be out of contact with the world that Friday at about noon for an hour or two, and could I get your mobile phone away from you just before then? He promised me two hundred pounds when he saw me next. Well, I never seed two hundred pounds in my life, Inspector. And I won't now, will I, seeing as how you've now got him inside.'

Angel picked up the pack of cigarettes and held onto them.

'I believe you know everything they get up to,' he said.

'No, sir. And that's the truth.'

'I believe you know where they meet.'

'No, sir,' he began. Then he hesitated. 'Well, er . . .'

Angel stared into his eyes. Spinetti stared back at him for a second then he began to blink. He blinked several times in quick succession and then looked downwards.

'Well, *where* do they meet, Sam?'

Angel waved the pack of cigarettes at him.

Spinetti looked at them momentarily transfixed.

'I don't *have* to tell anybody,' Angel said. 'Now. *Where do they meet?'*

'I don't seem to have any choice . . .'

Angel could see he was dithering. He ran a hand through his hair. 'For once in your life, Sam, do the decent thing. Tell the truth.'

Spinetti glanced at the pack of cigarettes in Angel's hand, pulled a tight face, rubbed his chin and very quietly said, 'The talk is that they meet in the hotel in Porley . . . it's a sort of a wee village between Ashton and Bromersley, don't you know? That's only what I have *heard*. It might not be right. But don't tell anybody you got that from me. And I don't know anything else, Inspector, honestly. Do I get the ciggies now?'

'And *when* do they meet?'

Spinetti swept an arm across his forehead to wipe off the perspiration.

'I don't know, Inspector!' he squealed.

Angel smiled. 'You never know your luck, Sam,' he said. 'You're not in here for long.'

'Me dear old mother didn't tell me life would be loike this.'

Angel stood up, still holding the pack of cigarettes, crossed the room, banged on the door and called, 'Officer.'

Spinetti said, 'Are you not going to give me the ciggies, Inspector, afore you go?'

Angel turned and put the pack into Spinetti's outstretched hand.

Spinetti handled the pack as if it was a two-hundred-year-old bone china cup. His face lit up. 'Oh thank you, Inspector. And God bless you.'

Angel was also quietly elated. He hadn't been as pleased for days. He reached to his top pocket and turned off the recorder. He hoped the miniature recorder had registered every word clearly.

* * *

There was a knock on the door of what used to be Angel's office.

'Come,' Detective Superintendent Fred Piggott said and prepared a toothy smile.

It was Angel.

'You wanted me, sir?'

'Aye. Come in. Sit down.'

Angel said, 'Are you making any progress, sir?'

'Yes. Yes. But not on the forensic evidence in front of me, Inspector,' Piggott said.

Angel gave a long sigh. 'All of that could be fixed if someone wanted me out of the way,' he said.

'I can't see that a judge and jury would see it that way.'

Angel ran a hand through his hair. 'Our house was broken into. We could find nothing important that had been taken—'

'I saw that, and as nothing had been taken—'

'The intruder could have — probably did — take a couple of hairs from my hair brushes and then rummaged through our dirty clothes basket and found a used handkerchief. We wouldn't miss items such as those, would we? That's why I was puzzled by the break-in.'

'The CPS don't see it like that, Angel. Their Mr Twelvetrees — you know him of course—'

'I certainly do.'

'He is very sympathetic to your position, but he can only foresee a guilty verdict.'

Angel was furious. He went red in the face. He jumped up. His eyes stuck out and showed the whites.

'Well, he *would,* wouldn't he?' he bawled. 'He's the leading barrister for the Crown *Prosecution* Service for round here.

He's the opposition. I consult him when I am having difficulty making a charge stick against a villain. *You* shouldn't even be *talking* to him.'

'Of course it is perfectly correct to be talking to him,' Piggott said. 'After all, he is representing police interests in this matter, and you *were* still a policeman at the time of these charges.'

Angel groaned and sat down. He held his head in his hands and shook it. After a few moments he looked up. 'Well who is representing me in court then?'

Piggott flashed his teeth in a smirk. 'His name is Thomas Goldberg, and I can promise he's the best you'll find . . . Happens to be an old crony of mine from college, you know. I've already briefed him on the ins and outs of your case, of course—'

Angel gasped. 'Oh no, you *haven't*. I want somebody who *knows* that I am innocent.'

'Well, if that's how you feel, I'm sure he'll gladly stand down,' Piggott sneered. 'But good luck getting another barrister stupid enough to take this case. What you really need, Angel, is somebody who can deliver a really good, original mitigation address.'

Angel's heart came up into his mouth. He began rocking in his chair . . . slightly backwards and then forwards and again and again and again. He swallowed several times, detected a sour taste, and licked his lips.

Piggott's eyebrows knitted together. He rubbed his temple as he watched Angel.

Eventually Angel stood up. He went out quickly, closed the door and made his way up the corridor past Harker's door to the end office. He knocked and went inside. A middle-aged woman with a sour expression was at a desk, pen in hand. She looked up over her horn-rimmed spectacles.

'I want to see the chief constable, please.'

'He's very busy, you know,' she said with her nose pointing up to the North Pole. 'Just a minute. What name is it?'

'DI Angel. It's extremely important.'

She stood up and went through a door in the wall behind her and closed it. A minute later, she returned carrying an open book, which Angel took to be a diary. Eventually she said, 'There's a ten-minute slot next Wednesday at—'

Angel shook his head. He didn't hear any more. He walked past her and opened the chief constable's office door.

The woman's face went scarlet. She rushed towards him, arms in the air.

'You can't go in *there*,' she said as she followed him in.

The chief constable had been reading a report at his desk. Hearing the disturbance, he looked up and saw Angel coming in, followed by his secretary.

The woman said to the chief, 'I couldn't stop him. He pushed straight past.'

The chief put up his hands to her to settle her down. 'That's all right, Mrs Witherspoon.'

Her mouth dropped open.

Angel said, 'Can I see you *now*, sir? It's *very* important.'

'It had better be,' the chief said.

The secretary was still waiting at the door.

'Do carry on with whatever you were doing, Mrs Witherspoon,' he said.

She looked at him, went out and closed the door.

The chief sat down and looked closely at the gatecrasher. The strain and distress on Angel's face were very evident to him.

The chief rubbed his chin. He caught Angel's eye and pointed to a chair.

Angel sat down opposite.

'What's the matter? Is the investigation not going well?'

Angel gave a slight shrug. 'It's not that, sir. It's the fact that I have only just understood that Superintendent Piggott's *mate* is to be my barrister in court?'

'Well, what's so wrong with that? He's fully qualified and has had plenty of experience and success in both civil and constabulary cases.'

Angel sighed. 'Even so, if he's in cahoots with Piggott, you can bet he believes I'm guilty of murdering Alfred Beecroft and is already pursuing a line of mitigation.'

'Yes, and he has approached me, and I have already given him a glowing account of your character and achievements. Also I have agreed to be a witness. You know, Angel, I have seen the evidence against you, and maybe this barrister thinks — with all his great experience at the bar — that this is the best course to take.'

Angel gasped. 'So you think I did it then?'

The chief said, 'I didn't say that at all. As a matter of fact, with your long and constant police record, I'm certain that you didn't.'

Angel was quiet for a few moments then he said, 'Thank you, sir. That means a lot. Well, anyway, I want you to replace this barrister with somebody who is or could be convinced of my innocence.'

The chief slowly stroked his chin with his fingertips. Eventually he said, 'The way things are, Michael, waiting for a replacement could take six months or even longer. The constabulary wouldn't pay your salary all that time. Also, if there's no one available on the books, could you afford to go the civil route — consult a solicitor and get *them* to come up with a barrister who suits your taste? The cost can be considerable, you know.'

Angel's face fell. He still had a mortgage on the bungalow, an overdraft with the bank, and owed several hundred pounds on his credit card. There was no way. He shook his head.

'No, sir,' he said. 'We could manage a couple of months. After that it would be difficult.'

'Are you making progress with your own investigations?'

'Slow, sir, but I am making good progress.'

'I suggest that when you get a rock-solid case together, present that to Superintendent Piggott and this barrister. I am sure they will both be delighted to accept it. That's what they're here for. In the meantime, I will have a private word with Piggott. And . . . well, let's take it from there.'

* * *

It was early morning on Wednesday, April 28.

Angel was in the bathroom looking in the mirror. He had stuck a false moustache on his top lip. He was checking that it was in position and that it looked like the genuine article. When he was satisfied, he put on a pair of spectacles with imitation tortoiseshell frames and clear-glass lenses.

Then he turned to the full-length mirror, checking to see that the tartan kilt he wore was hanging evenly. Then he put on a Harris tweed sports jacket, took another glance in the mirror, nodded and walked confidently into the kitchen.

Mary was finishing off her breakfast while reading the paper. She looked up, frowned, then smiled. 'What have you dragged that old Scotland the Brave kit out for?'

'Don't mock it, sweetheart. It has served me very well over the years. If you must know, I'm going on a fishing trip.'

'You need a rod and a wee stool then.' She grinned.

'Not that kind of trip, my dear. Fishing for information. And I think I've got the bait for it.'

* * *

Angel soon found the tiny village of Porley. Two streets, one closed-down corner shop and one pub, the Travellers. It was a big stone-faced building on the main road, and really more like a hotel.

Angel parked the BMW in the car park and made his way into the hotel. Inside was even more grandiose than the exterior suggested.

He saw a sign illuminating the word 'Reception' above an alcove by the door. Behind the counter, a young woman was tapping into a computer.

He leaned over the counter and, adopting a Scottish twang, said, 'Excuse me, miss.'

She looked up from the screen. 'Can I help you?'

'Aye. You can that. Do you have a wee room for a dozen or so Scottish friends to meet for a conference — and maybe a drink or two, you ken?'

'Yes, sir,' she said. 'Which date did you have in mind?'

'We'd like to meet on the same day every month — such as, the second Tuesday in the month or the first Wednesday — so that members dinnae forget.'

She smiled. 'A series booking. I understand. Excuse me while I find the book.'

She reached down to somewhere under the counter.

A glass bowl sat on the counter, filled with books of matches advertising the hotel. Angel picked one out.

The young lady came up with a big book.

He waved the matches at her. 'Is this free?'

'Of course,' she grinned.

'I'll take it then, and thank ye.'

The clerk opened the book at the present week.

Angel began to exercise his skill at reading upside down. He observed the entries. There was one for the TWA, whatever that was, at two o'clock the following day.

He said, 'Now, miss, I dinnae suppose it would be free tomorrow afternoon?'

'No, I'm sorry.'

'Oh?' Angel sniffed. 'It's not another Scottish club trying to pip me at the post, is it? It'll be young Willy McTavish of the Caledonians Club, I expect.'

'No, sir,' she said, her nose in the air. 'It's a Mr Oscar Starr of the TWA.'

That set Angel thinking. That would be the little crook, the accountant he already knew about. He wondered what TWA stood for.

The clerk turned the page. Angel could see that there were two weddings on the Friday and Saturday, followed by another meeting of the TWA the following Thursday.

The clerk flicked forward a few pages. 'Thursdays, Saturdays and Sundays are out, but it looks as if the other days are free.'

Angel feigned disappointment. 'Hmm. I'd better see the room before I go any further. If you dinnae mind?'

'Of course,' she said and banged a push-down bell on the countertop. She turned to a board hung with keys at her side, took one down, and then looked across the foyer expectantly. Nothing happened. Nobody came.

'There should be a porter around . . .'

She banged the bell again. There was still no response.

She sighed. 'I'll take you myself, sir. If you will follow me.'

'I'm right behind ye, ma lady,' he said.

The room was a short trek along a corridor on the ground floor.

She unlocked a door.

Angel followed her into the room and glanced around. It was small and pleasantly decorated. There were about twenty chairs and two six-foot-long tables stacked up tidily in one corner.

'We would put the chairs and tables wherever you want them, of course,' the clerk said.

'Aye. Thank ye for that, miss.' Turning his attention to the windows, Angel pretended to consider the view.

At that moment, a man in tails put his head round the door and said something quietly to the reception clerk before rushing away.

She hesitated, then said, 'I'm wanted on the phone, sir. Will you excuse me a couple of minutes?'

'Of course,' Angel said. 'I'll have wee look round. Dinnae hurry back on my account.'

She smiled and went breezing out of the room.

He was glad of her absence because he had something he wanted to do secretly.

He closed the door and wedged a chair under the handle. He looked up at the ceiling and noted the imposing decorative light fitting holding ten lamps shaped like flowers in bud.

Perfect. He pulled one of the tables to the middle of the room, directly underneath the light fitting. He then put a chair on the table. Then he mounted the table and stood on the chair. When he was up there, he pulled a matchbox out of his pocket. Inside it was a tiny torpedo-shaped object made of plastic, fastened to a piece of brown paper. It was a cleverly made recording device. He pressed the end to activate it, peeled off the brown paper to reveal an adhesive surface and then stuck it on the inside of the fitting, out of sight and also out of any direct heat from the lamps.

Then he heard the door handle rattle, several times and very rapidly.

'Are you in there, sir?' The clerk's voice called out. 'Is anybody in there?'

He leaped down and quickly placed the furniture back where it had been. Then he removed the chair he had used to wedge the door shut and rattled the handle several times. 'Can you hear me?'

'Yes.'

'Try the door now, miss,' Angel said. 'It seems a bit stiff.'

The door opened and in she came like a tornado.

She looked hastily around the room to see what might be different. Then she glared at Angel and said, 'Were you holding the door against me?'

'No,' he said. 'I was mysel' trying to open it. Well, I'll be on my way, miss. Thank you for your attention. I'll consult with my committee and be in touch.'

TWELVE

30 Park Drive, Forest Hill Estate, Bromersley, South Yorkshire
Thursday, 29 April, 7.30 a.m.

Next day, Angel had discarded the kilt, moustache and all other things Scottish. He came into the kitchen that morning in his usual dark suit, white shirt, collar and tie.

Mary looked up at him. 'Are you going to tangle with the Velleman gang then? Putting yourself in harm's way *again*?'

Angel didn't want to say yes, and he didn't want to lie. The fact that he hesitated, though, told Mary that it was indeed his intention.

Her face went white. She squeezed the handle of the teacup she was holding then banged it back in its saucer.

'Oh, Michael!'

'Well, I *have* to get that journal back,' he said. 'And I think they must have it.'

'But you said you didn't see who knocked you out.'

'I didn't, but it must have been Fellowes or somebody from the fairground, because that's where I was. And Brian Fellowes' circumstances have altered. His rich wife has finally left him. So now he will be compelled to earn more money very quickly.'

'What's Fellowes' wife got to do with it?'

'Well, apparently it was *her* money that was supporting Fellowes' business. Now he'll have to concentrate on replenishing his finances and I wouldn't be surprised if he starts by selling the journal to Alexander Velleman.'

'Is Brian Fellowes a member of Velleman's gang then?'

'Not sure. But he certainly knows *some* of them,' he said looking at his watch. 'Must go,' he said. 'You haven't forgotten about our code, have you? What to do if *the goldfish* needs feeding . . .'

'Of course not,' she said irritably.

'I want you to add another name to that list.'

'Oh, Michael.'

'Listen to me, sweetheart. It's Detective Inspector Harris of Greater Manchester Police. The number is on the pad. He knows Velleman's address. Have you got that?'

She put her hands on her hips and breathed in noisily through her nose. 'Yes, yes, yes!' she said. 'DI Harris of Greater Manchester Police. Another name on the list.'

Then he pulled her to him, wrapped his arms round her, and gave her the gentlest, sweetest kiss.

As she pulled away, Mary looked stunned. Then her face turned white. She grabbed his arm. 'Oh, don't go, Michael,' she said. There was a tremor in her voice. 'Those men are dangerous.'

'I've got to, darling. I've got to get that book. I've got to clear my name. I'll be back before you know it.'

Mary shuddered then said, 'Oh, Michael.' Her eyes were overly bright because they were wet with tears.

* * *

It was ten minutes to two on Thursday afternoon when Angel arrived back in Porley.

He had checked over the miniature recorder in his top pocket, inserted a blank tape and new batteries. He couldn't afford to miss any supporting evidence that might be released in the course of the day.

He drove the BMW into the Travellers' hotel car park and noted the presence of a familiar vintage Rolls-Royce parked near the side door of the hotel.

As he looked for a suitable parking place, where he could be inconspicuous among a bunch of other cars yet able to observe the Rolls-Royce, he didn't fail to notice a navy-blue car drive in behind him. Two men were seated in the front, but its rear windows were blacked out. It had followed him into the car park and parked in a space close to the exit.

Angel found a suitable space and reversed into it. He switched off the engine, opened the small locker under the dashboard, and took out a miniaturised shortwave receiver/recorder, two lengths of insulated wire and a pair of earphones. He set them up on the car seat, connecting them, and taking power from the cigarette lighter socket.

In a couple of minutes, he was recording and simultaneously listening to the meeting of the gang, who were no more than two hundred yards and a stone wall away. He snuggled down in the car seat and closed his eyes as he wanted to concentrate on what was happening and what was being said.

* * *

The usual handwritten sign hung on the meeting-room door. *The Tiddlywinks Association. Private. Members only.*

Ten men of various ages in lounge suits, collars and ties were assembled in the room. Along one side was a rectangular table, and two men were seated behind it. On the white-cloth-covered table in front of them were two boxes of tiddlywinks, with coloured counters surrounding them. The members were clicking away at the counters, ostensibly trying to get them into the cups.

A waiter with a tray was circulating the room, delivering drinks and collecting dirty glasses.

There was a strange silence among the members.

The waiter, having served everyone, crossed to the big man at the table. 'Will there be anything else, sir?'

'No. Leave us,' Velleman said, taking a fat cigar out of his mouth and waving an impatient arm.

The waiter went out, watched by almost everybody.

As soon as the door closed behind him, the two men pretending to play the game dropped the act and moved to sit with the others.

Velleman produced a single sheet of paper from his pocket and without any preamble said, 'First of all, I call on Mr Starr to make an important announcement.'

* * *

Angel, listening in his car, was delighted at the clarity of the speech he was receiving through the headphones and hoped his recording was as clear.

* * *

Small, bald Oscar Starr was the other man seated at the table with Velleman. He stood up while putting on his glasses and said, 'Oh, yes. That very dangerous book, a diary of some of our activities of late, written by that stupid woman Gloria Van Haven, was obtained by us very late last night. I'm pleased to say we got it after several thwarted attempts.'

There were a few claps. The applause increased until everybody was clapping.

As the applause waned, Starr held up the book for everybody to see.

'I told you gentlemen I'd stop at nothing to lay my hands on this — and here it is,' he said. 'The journal that has caused all the trouble. I can't think of anything more stupid than committing to paper the times, dates and places of where we did each job. It's like writing a personal request to go to prison for twenty-five years. Anyway, you'll be pleased to hear that it will be destroyed . . . burned to ashes.'

He turned to look at Velleman, who nodded approvingly.

There were calls of 'Hurray' and 'Not before time.'

Starr leaned over to Velleman. 'Do you want to say anything about that, Alex?'

Velleman thought a moment and then stood up.

'You will be pleased to know that the man who had possession of the journal, a man called Brian Fellowes, has had his bits chopped off. I had the pleasure of wielding the scalpel. He subsequently died, and his remains were dumped in the river.'

At that, there was heartier applause, including banging on chair arms, whistling, and shouts of 'hurray,' 'serve the bastard right!' and 'good old Alex!'

When the applause stopped, Alexander Velleman stood up and said, 'Thank you, thank you.' He smiled at them. 'Now that that's out of the way, is there any other business?'

Dr William Hart, who was seated by the window, also stood up. 'Yes. I have a point, Alex. You got me out of custody, for which I am eternally grateful, but James Robertson and Sebastian are still in Manchester nick. We ought to be doing something about getting *them* out. Now that we have more handguns than we need, why don't we increase our number and take on much bigger—'

He was interrupted by Oscar Starr, who jumped up and said, 'That would require us engaging in the tedious and risky business of checking out new faces. That costs even more and takes up a lot of time. And we can't be doing that on the cheap. We always run the risk of recruiting a police spy. In addition, it would reduce our payout percentage. I wouldn't want to go down that path yet. The executives have this at the front of their minds and are working on it, but we also have to protect our capital reserves, which I must remind you are low.'

He sat down.

Hart stood up again. 'I appreciate what you say, Mr Starr, but if the gang was bigger, we could also do more risky jobs because there would be more of us, and we would be armed which would enable us to take on the cops.'

Velleman turned. 'You are wasting time, Mr Hart. Mr Starr has already told you that he, others and myself are working on this. And you have heard, it would be an expensive operation to mount. It would be better if you spent your time searching for easier jobs that produce big rewards for us instead of suggesting ways of spending our very limited funds unnecessarily. Now, is there any other—'

'That's not fair!' Hart's face was scarlet and he had jumped to his feet.

'Sit down, Hart,' Velleman said heavily. 'And shut your mouth.'

Hart hesitated. He glanced around the stony faces of the men at the table and the others in the room and realised that nobody was brave enough to support him, so he sat down and folded his arms. He had a face like thunder and his heart was pounding like a Salvation Army drum.

Velleman said, 'If there is no more business from the floor, I have an item. I will remind members that every word spoken in this room, and out of it, about our organisation is top secret. You all know that. I have said it before. If anyone utters a word about this organisation outside of this room, I will personally castrate him before I kill him.'

Velleman's tiny mean eyes looked round the room at each member in turn to indicate that the threat included them.

He said, 'Take Gloria Van Haven, the only woman member we have had for a good while. She was planning to leak information about our organisation to a troublesome copper, so I instructed James Robertson to cut out her womb before killing her and dispatching her to the river.'

There were cheers, strange howling noises and cries of 'Wow!' and 'Great job.'

When the noises of approval quietened, Angel heard Starr say, 'I've nothing else, Alex.'

Velleman said, 'That's it, gentlemen. The meeting is over. We meet here same time next week.'

He turned to Starr. 'Are you going to pay the bill now?'

'Yes, I'll see you in the car.'

'Shall I take the book?'

'No. It's all right. I'll only be two minutes.'

* * *

Angel pulled out the earphones. His pulse was racing. His chest was burning. He was sickened by what he'd heard — the gory details of Gloria Van Haven's killing, and the gang's thirst for torture and murder. But he had also noted that Oscar Starr had the journal and intended on burning it. He would have to retrieve it before it went up in smoke.

His attention was suddenly drawn to some activity at the rear door of the hotel. He had to sit up and lean forward in the BMW to see as much as possible of the back door and the Rolls.

He saw Velleman come out of the back door, draped in a long black overcoat and Homburg hat. The big man opened the side door of the limousine and climbed inside.

Angel recalled Starr saying that he would only take two minutes. He got out of the car and, in a semi-crouch, ran towards the Rolls. He edged round the back and waited.

He was just in time.

Oscar Starr came out of the back door carrying the journal close to his chest.

Angel leaped at him, grabbed the book, pushed him over onto the stone flags and then raced through the car-park exit.

Velleman rushed out of the Rolls and went over to help Starr to his feet.

The two men in the navy-blue car saw everything that happened. As Angel raced by, he noticed that they looked at each other in surprise.

The way to his car — and a quick getaway — was blocked, and Angel had no idea where he was headed as he barrelled out of the car park. He crossed the road and spotted a wooden farm gate. Gripping it with his free hand, he leaped over it into a field. It had a haystack in the corner. He stopped behind it briefly to consider where he was going. He heard two gunshots behind him. It spurred him on to run faster in any direction away from the gunfire.

That direction turned out to be north-east, Angel realised. The sun was shining, giving him a sense of direction. He ran through ploughed fields, flocks of sheep and herds of cows. He jumped or climbed over gates, stone walls and fences. He aimed to keep to fields and woodland, where cars could not follow.

He ran until he could run no more. He slumped down on one knee against a stone wall, panting. His heart was thumping away as loud as a Sousa march. He relaxed his grip on the red book and tried to think straight. He looked round for a farm building, barn or shelter where he could hide it — a landmark he could hark back to. But all the fields looked similar and he didn't know the area.

Suddenly he glimpsed the top of the old Rolls-Royce over a wall in the next field, around three hundred yards away.

Angel caught his breath. His hands gripped the book. He dropped to the ground, lying full-length in the shade of the wall, as still as a corpse. *There must be a road or track of some sort nearby*. He just hadn't realised it.

The car seemed to be travelling at around 20 mph. The bulky head and shoulders of Velleman were sticking out of the top — his binoculars trained outwards — like a military-tank commander.

Angel stayed on the ground until the Rolls had gone. On his knees, he peeked over the stone wall. At the other side of the next field was a cluster of trees. It looked like an area of woodland. He couldn't see how far it extended, but it would give him more shelter than an open field.

He looked cautiously around. There was no sign of life. He climbed over the stone wall, disturbing several grazing sheep who began running away from him.

Somehow, Angel made it to the woods. Once inside, he pushed his way through brambles, fallen trunks and weeds towards a dense growth of trees — grown so tall and straight that they shut out the sun. Without the light from the sky, the wood became eerily dull.

As he pushed his way further into the wood, he was still considering where to hide the book. He didn't want to lose it again. It was too valuable. Also, he did not want to hide it in a place and then not be able to find it. He hoped for . . . an outbuilding or a statue or an unusual natural phenomenon like a waterfall, but there was nothing.

It was just at that point that he heard the snapping of twigs behind him and a man's voice. He froze on the spot. To his side, he saw a rotting fallen tree with a clump of toadstools growing on it. The silver birch had fallen on uneven ground and there was space under it that would partly conceal him. He grabbed a long piece of bracken, dropped down to the leaf-covered ground, slid under the tree and pulled the bracken over his face.

As the snapping of twigs grew louder, Angel's heartbeat got faster.

He could hear the heavy breathing of a man.

The rubber heel of a large leather shoe trod briefly on compacted leaves ten centimetres from Angel's head.

He held his breath and closed his eyes. His muscles tightened. The banging of his heart seemed deafening.

The owner of the shoe moved on. 'I could have sworn I heard somebody.'

Angel had no idea who it could be — if not another of Velleman's bully boys.

'You can bet it was that bastard Angel,' another voice said.

'If we don't get that bloody book back, I will have to emigrate.'

'Emigrate! Where to?' the first man said breathlessly.

'I don't know,' the man said as he climbed over the dead tree. 'But I have no intention of doing another stretch in the pokey.'

'Me neither.'

'I hear there's easy money to be had in South America.'

'That's a hell of a long way to go. I'm not sure I could get Emma to go with me.'

'Leave her, then. In Rio de Janeiro there are thousands of women . . .'

Angel didn't hear the end of that sentence.

He sighed with relief and waited several minutes until the two villains were well out of sight. Then he eased himself out from under the log, sat on it and took out his phone. He found the super's number and tapped on it.

Harker answered. Angel explained the situation he was in, but Harker didn't seem to appreciate the value of the book, or the urgency of Angel's predicament.

'That's all supposition and hearsay, Angel. Who's to say that book isn't full of lies anyway? If what you say is true, this Gloria wasn't exactly a reliable witness. Now, when you get back to the station, Angel, come in to see me. *I* will evaluate the new evidence you have with Superintendent Piggott and some decisions can perhaps be made then. Does that satisfy you?'

'No, sir. I need some help *now*, urgently — if I'm to get safely out of this wood with this book. The Velleman gang are armed and I'm not. And they're closing in on me.'

'I think you are exaggerating, Angel,' Harker said. 'Anyway, what can I possibly do to help?'

'You could send an armed unit to meet me at the Travellers' Hotel in Porley.'

'That's not on our patch, is it? We would either have to ask Manchester to send out a team, or at least seek their permission to enter their patch.'

'You know that these permissions are more of a courtesy than anything else! And in an emergency like this is, they can easily be executed retrospectively.'

'Look, Angel, you're forgetting that you are not in the force now. You're just a civilian, an ordinary member of the public. I can't be summoning armed officers out on the whim of a member of the public. You are *that* pumped up with your own self-importance, man. What possible interest could that gang have in you now that you are *not* a policeman? Come in and see me when you get back.'

Then the line went dead.

Angel was well aware that Harker had always envied his popularity with the press and the complimentary headlines he sometimes received after solving a particularly unusual or interesting case, but he didn't expect that attitude from the man. Not when a fellow officer and human being was in such a life-threatening situation.

Angel wrinkled his nose and pocketed his mobile. He would have to accept the fact that he was on his own. He could phone DS Carter. She would do what she could. She could bring a car and whisk him out of the place. They'd just have to hope they weren't followed . . . but he wasn't able to give her a meeting place that would be safe. She couldn't bring a gun anyway. Harker would never agree to that.

Angel thought about the situation a minute or so longer.

He made a decision.

He quickly sat back down on the fallen tree and removed one of his shoes and a sock. He put his shoe back on. He stood up and wandered round the immediate area of the wood looking at the ground. From time to time he made scraping movements with his foot, rather like an angry bull before it charges at the matador. Eventually he kicked a heap of leaves angrily into the air and gave the scraping up. He put the sock in his pocket and ran a hand through his hair. In some small way, it helped him to tolerate the situation.

He wanted to hide the book. He thought of wrapping it in the sock but he had a better idea for that item of clothing. He looked around for possible places but came back to the log that had successfully part-concealed himself. He pressed the book into a crevice under the log, and then kicked and pushed fallen leaves over and around it. Then he stood back and looked at the scene. Even if the leaves were blown away, the book would still be impossible to find without foreknowledge. And if he could get things sorted quickly enough the book would not get too damp in the ground.

He made the decision to leave it where it was, and make the best effort to get himself safely back home.

He then made his way back to the edge of the wood and looked out. He wanted to remember the view. In the middle distance he saw a trail of grey pylons in the evening sunlight. He would remember them in relation to where he was standing. He looked and listened. It was pleasantly quiet and still. He stepped out from the shelter of the wood into the big open field of sheep. He *could* stick to the perimeter — and the relative safety of the stone wall's cover — but that would mean running the longer distance. So he nervously ran the much shorter trip straight across the field, disturbing a few grazing sheep, who scattered obligingly out of his way. He climbed the low stone wall, which put him in the corner of a ploughed field. He squatted there. It was a place of relative safety. There was a bush in the corner providing some cover. Angel rested there and listened. At first he could hear only the gentle wind . . . then he heard the gentle tinkling of running water. It came from the field behind him. He could do with a drink. He stood up, peered over the wall and saw a small stream of water running all the way down the field. He climbed over the wall, cupped his hands and caught several hands full of clear, cool water, and drank it. Then he began to pull out one of the smooth, hard stones, one the water could have been running over for many years. He held it up to the red setting sunlight. It was about six centimetres in diameter. He weighed it in his hand like a cricket ball and smiled. It was heavy for its volume. *Just what he wanted.*

From his pocket, he took out the sock. He put the stone in it and shook it to the bottom. Holding the sock at the top, he swung the heavy stone around as fast as he could generating a serious thrust. Nodding with satisfaction, he tucked his new weapon in his pocket with the neck of the sock sticking out.

He thought he heard a rustling sound nearby. It wasn't trees. It was the sound that some raincoats make as the wearer moves around. The sound was getting louder. Angel couldn't move. Goosebumps ran up and down his arms. The sound stopped over the wall in the place he had occupied a minute ago.

The silhouette of a man appeared above the top of the wall in the next field. He was holding a handgun.

'Ah! Inspector Angel,' the man said. 'Stand up, where I can see you.'

Angel peered at him through the fading light and recognised him immediately. Dr William Hart.

'Inspector Angel. We meet again. But this time is better. It's my turn to get my own back. I have been looking forward to this. Come back over the wall . . . and bring that diary with you.'

As Angel climbed over the wall, Hart looked him up and down, somewhat agitated.

'Where is it?' he said.

Angel looked at him as expressionless as he could manage.

'Put your hands up. Is it over the wall?' Hart said.

Angel didn't reply.

'Open your coat,' Hart said.

Angel stared at the gun, trying to think of a way of relieving Hart of it.

Hart waved it at him and screamed, 'I said, open your coat!'

Angel very deliberately lowered his hands, unfastened the button on his suit jacket, and opened both sides wide — thankful that he was no longer carrying Gloria's diary.

Hart pressed his lips together. 'Have you left it over there?'

Still, Angel said nothing.

Hart's lips tightened. He took one step closer to Angel and stared into his eyes.

'Have you left it over there?' he bawled, clenching and unclenching his free hand. 'Are you deaf or dumb or something? I saw you fiddling about in that corner. Digging with your hands or something. Have you buried it there?'

Angel remained silent.

Hart pushed Angel out of his way and climbed the low wall. Halfway over, he turned back to Angel. 'Put your hands up and no funny business. It would give me great pleasure to kill you. Remember this gun goes off very easily. If you're thinking of running, I wouldn't bother. Lead from this gun can fly faster than you can. All right?'

Hart dropped out of sight for a moment behind the wall. He bobbed straight back to see if Angel had moved. Satisfied, he bent back down checking the fresh earth round the stream. He found it difficult in the fading light.

With the speed of a missile, Angel pulled out the sock with the stone in the foot, leaned over the wall and swung the home-made weapon hard at Hart's temple.

Hart gasped then went down like a playing card tower in an earthquake. He made an ungainly motionless heap in the corner of the field.

Angel exhaled a lungful of air, stuffed the weapon back in his pocket, and quickly scaled the wall. He saw Hart's gun glinting in the grass where it had fallen. He reached down for it. Squeezed the grip. It felt good. He checked the magazine. It was fully loaded and there was a bullet in the barrel. He checked the safety catch and pushed it into his pocket.

He looked at the victim. Hart was motionless and his breathing seemed normal. He would come round soon.

He must press on.

Angel climbed back over the wall and raced down the perimeter of the field. In the fading light, he saw that the field was seeded with a grain of some sort.

The next was fallow and had a haystack covered with canvas in the corner. One side of the field had a hedge running down it, mostly constituted of hawthorn and some bushes. In the middle of the hedge was a five-barred gate.

Suddenly, Angel remembered where he was. It was the first gate he had leaped over when he was running away from Starr with Gloria's book. The gate was directly opposite the hotel car park.

He stopped, pushed his way into a bush and went down on one knee. Pressing down a branch, he saw the hotel lights illuminating the car park and the roadway.

He looked across at the car park. All was quiet and still. He was relieved to see his BMW, exactly where he'd left it among twenty or thirty other cars. His eyes also caught the shape of the Rolls-Royce sitting proudly by the back door, its usual parking spot. He wondered whether Velleman would have positioned gunmen or look-outs to observe his BMW. He reasoned that that would depend on the men he had available. Angel decided, based on the number of men he had heard at the meeting, that he probably would.

He made a decision. He needed a diversion. It depended on whether he had that book of matches he had picked up at the hotel reception desk the day before. He fished in his pocket and found it there.

He knew exactly what he was going to do. He made his way twenty yards back to the haystack in the corner of the field, took out the matches and set fire to it. There was a slight breeze, which helped fan the flames. The fire spread quickly and when Angel thought the time was right, he took out the gun, pointed it skyward and pulled the trigger. He fired three shots.

Then he ran up the length of the field, and over a gate through to the next field, still keeping to the hedge that ran parallel to the road.

Looking through a gap in the hedge, he saw four men emerge from the car park and run across the road towards the fire. Seconds later, Starr and Velleman appeared through the back door of the hotel and gazed up at the blaze.

Angel took his opportunity. He ran a little further along in the hedge bottom to a gate. He looked round. There didn't seem to be anybody about, so he climbed over that, ran across the open road to the hedge at the other side and then made his way from the other side of the road back towards the car park.

Ahead, he could see four men standing in the road looking at the fire. Then he saw Velleman strut out to them. He called out a command and waved his arm in the direction of the fire. He had been instructing them to go into the field, presumably to learn more about the cause of the fire and the reason for the gunshots.

Angel looked for Starr but he was nowhere to be seen.

A few villagers and some people who were visiting the hotel had arrived, and were standing in the road staring at the fire, which had quickly become quite wild and ferocious in the breeze.

With all eyes looking in that direction, Angel had no difficulty in reaching the car park unobserved. He made his way to his car, unlocked the door, started the engine, and drove slowly and quietly down towards the exit.

Just at that moment, the back door of the hotel opened and little Oscar Starr came through it. When he saw Angel in the BMW, his eyes and mouth opened wide and he reached out to the car, fumbling for something to grab hold of. He caught a door handle but soon let go as Angel slammed his foot down on the accelerator.

Angel tore out of the car park and onto the road. He heard three gunshots in quick succession behind him. He was not aware that they had hit the BMW. The tyres gave a squeal as Angel pressed the car to go even faster.

He drove for a mile or so before switching on the headlights. He turned on to the main road to Sheffield, then headed for Bromersley and home.

THIRTEEN

The road across the moors wasn't busy. Angel put his foot down and attempted to break every speed limit to put distance between himself and the mob. He had already covered ten miles when he found the car was not running to its usual standard. It was sluggish, and the steering felt wrong, so he looked for a side road where it would be safe to stop and try to see what might be wrong. He found a quiet lane where he turned off and travelled down a hundred metres or so. He stopped, turned off the lights and got out of the car. He flashed his torchlight at the tyres and found that he had a puncture. He had no pump, but he did have a spare wheel which was in good order.

He made the change, turned the car round and returned to the main road. He tested the car out at up to eighty miles an hour and it ran perfectly well. He reckoned that that had lost him about twenty minutes all in.

He could see no persistent lights in his rear mirror, so he was hoping he was not being followed. He had about thirty miles more to travel so he could be home in less than an hour. The clock on the dashboard told him it was eight o'clock. He was looking forward to seeing Mary.

Suddenly the car gave a *ping-ping* sound, and the petrol pump icon flashed up on the dash.

Angel looked at the fuel gauge, gave a growling sound and scrubbed a hand across his face. He would have to stop at a service station. And soon.

The road twisted and turned and, as he gained height, surmounting the Pennines, he ran into clouds of night mist that slowed him down.

He drove another four miles or so and wondered how much further the car would travel before it came slithering to a halt.

After taking another bend in the road, through the pitch black of the night, he saw bright lights ahead. He sighed and smiled when he saw that it was a service station.

Much relieved, he turned off the main road and drove the car up to a pump.

He put the nozzle into the petrol tank of the BMW and squeezed the handle. He usually filled the tank, but time was precious. Twenty pounds' worth would be sufficient to see him home.

He went into the kiosk, paid the attendant, and stuffed the receipt in his wallet as he rushed across the forecourt.

When he reached his car, he heard a heavy, ponderous voice behind him say, 'Mr Angel, I am pointing a gun at you. Turn round very slowly.'

Angel's mouth fell open. His heart dropped down to his stomach. He recognised the voice. It was that of Alexander Velleman.

Then in front of him he saw the vintage Rolls-Royce pull slowly, silently onto the forecourt, followed by a black Mercedes. Both vehicles stopped, the doors opened, and the drivers and passengers tumbled quickly out. There were eight men in total. They lined up against the brick wall with guns drawn and pointed at Angel.

The largest gathering in the north of England for some years of the most evil collection of murderers and crooks in the business.

From behind a petrol pump, Velleman said, 'I hope that you will accept my most cordial invitation to come to my house for supper?'

Angel could hear his heart throbbing in his ear. 'Do I have a choice?'

Velleman said, 'By the way, I do believe that you have found a gun that probably dropped out of Dr Hart's pocket when you two were . . . chatting together earlier. Well, it belongs to me. And I am most eager to have it back. It's part of a set, you see. I am sure you will be anxious to return it.'

Angel knew he would have to surrender it. If he didn't offer it up now, Velleman would have him searched.

Angel put his hand in his jacket pocket.

'Please hold it by the barrel, Mr Angel,' Velleman said. 'I wouldn't want it to go off by accident and hurt anybody. Put it carefully on the floor. Thank you.'

A hand appeared and picked up the gun.

Angel's muscles tensed as he was led into Velleman's evil world.

Surrendering the gun was not a move he had wanted to make. If he had kept the gun, he might have been able to pick off Velleman and Starr before he was himself killed by the others.

He knew what was in Velleman's mind. When the big man had extricated every little bit of information he wanted out of Angel, he would kill him. That was why he no longer cared to conceal his place of residence, his identity and the identity of others in his gang. *When you're going to be murdered, it doesn't matter what you know. You are not going to be in a position to tell anybody.*

'Now then, Mr Angel, please join me in my limousine. I have instructed my most experienced driver to follow behind us in your car.'

The little chauffeur got out of the Rolls, opened the back door and with an open hand invited Angel to enter.

Angel peered inside and saw Starr seated in the back next to the opposite window. Starr looked at him then turned his face away. Angel sat next to him anyway. Velleman sat nearest the other window so that Angel was in the middle.

'Home, Jack, and make it quick,' Velleman called out to the chauffeur.

'At once,' the little man replied.

Velleman looked at Angel and put on a false smile.

Angel was deep in thought. He knew that if he allowed himself to be taken to Velleman's house he was as good as dead, and he hadn't been expecting to meet Saint Peter at the pearly gates quite so early.

* * *

About two hours later . . .

Angel was thinking. He looked away from the log fire momentarily and glanced around the sitting room. The house wasn't a house. It was a mansion. Like a little piece of Buckingham Palace. And the meal wasn't a meal. It was a banquet. A five-course banquet.

He was in a chair next to Velleman. The man was smoking a Churchill-sized cigar and swilling a brandy in the giant glass cupped in his hand.

'Now then, Mr Angel,' he said. 'What's on your mind?'

'I was thinking that it's getting late and I haven't phoned my wife. She'll be worried about me.'

'We can soon put that right. Please be so kind as to press that bell on the wall there.'

Angel pressed the button.

'We should be making for our beds soon, Mr Angel. You will be spending a night in a guest room here, of course, and then early in the morning we will go and pick up Gloria Van Haven's diary.'

Angel wondered if he should protest. It might look sharp practice if he let the assumption go unchallenged.

'I won't be able to do that, Mr Velleman,' he said.

The big man slowly took the cigar out of his mouth and pursed his thick lips. 'Oh, I think you *will*, Mr Angel. I think you will.'

Angel frowned. He wondered what to reply.

He was still wondering when the chauffeur came in.

Little Jack had swapped his blue-grey buttoned up coat for a short white coat. He crossed the room to Velleman.

'Mr Angel wants to send a message to his wife,' Velleman said, then he looked at Angel. 'Jack will get the number and deliver a short message.'

Angel gave him his home number and said, 'Tell her I am sorry I won't be home tonight. That everything is OK and ask her not to forget to feed the goldfish. That last bit is important. I am very fond of Nemo.'

'I'll do it straightaway,' the little man said.

Velleman said, 'Then come back here, Jack. Mr Angel is retiring. I want you to take him to the guest room.'

Jack nodded and left the room.

* * *

Standing outside the bedroom door was a villain Angel already knew. It was the fair-haired Hans. They exchanged glances of mutual wariness and hatred.

Hans turned around, took a key from his pocket and unlocked the door.

Angel noticed that Hans rotated the key twice on unlocking the door. Angel knew that the first rotation locked the door around the middle edge of the door in the usual way. The second turn operated additional locks at the top and bottom of the door for extra strength. In addition, he noticed that the door was almost double the usual thickness. He would need a miracle to escape through there.

Jack went in first. Hans followed Angel and Jack into the room.

It was a big room furnished with an old double bed, two huge wardrobes with full-length mirrors in the doors, two bedside tables and a tallboy.

Angel was fascinated by the beautifully turned, matching carved posts at each corner of the bed. The knobs at the top were a bit bigger than cricket balls.

Jack also showed Angel the en-suite bathroom. Then he said, 'Pyjamas under the pillow, slippers and dressing gown in the wardrobe. If you want anything in the night, just pick up the phone. All right?'

Angel nodded.

Jack went out.

Hans said, 'Get undressed and give me your clothes.'

'What for?'

'So that they can be laundered and freshly pressed for tomorrow.'

Angel wrinkled his nose. 'There's no need for that. They'll be all right as they are.'

'It's not optional, Angel,' Hans said. *'Get them off.'*

Angel rubbed his chin. He tried not to show his feelings as the gang took away his liberty piece by piece.

'It's to stop me running off in the night, isn't it?'

'That's not even possible. There's bars on the windows in the bathroom as well as in the bedroom. And when I've got your clothes, I will be locking the door. And, as a matter of interest, if you haven't yet noticed, there are cameras in both rooms, so we always know what you're up to.'

Angel took out his mobile and miniature recording machine and put them on the bedside table. He removed his coat, dropped it on the bed and reached up to slacken off his tie.

Hans promptly leaned forward, picked up the coat, and put the phone and the recorder back in the pockets.

Angel's lips tightened. 'I might need those.'

'We'll see to all your needs,' Hans said. 'Just pick up the phone. Meanwhile, we'll make sure the batteries are fully charged for you for tomorrow.'

Angel glared at him. That was obvious rubbish. But now was not the time to make a stand. He took several deep breaths, fighting to keep his cool. But his pulse was still speeding. His heartbeat still pounding.

Hans put the coat over his arm and waited for Angel's tie, shirt, trousers and shoes. Then he finally left.

Angel heard the *click* as he locked the door behind him.

He looked down at himself in vest, pants and socks. He turned back the pillow and found a pair of pyjamas, which he put on over his underwear. Then took a pair of slippers and a dressing gown from the wardrobe.

While he was by one of the wardrobes, he looked carefully at the big mirror, the way it was fixed to the door and at the screws in the hinges.

Then he went to the bathroom, had a good wash and searched the cabinet over the sink. There among the new toothbrushes, toothpaste and razors, he spotted a small nail file and surreptitiously transferred it to the dressing-gown pocket in a way that would have made Houdini proud.

He returned to the bedroom, picked up the battery clock on the bedside table, and pressed the bar across the top. A dim light illuminated the dial. He grinned.

Aware that he was in full glare of a camera, he took off the dressing gown and slippers, pulled back the duvet, and sat on the edge of the bed. He swung his legs round, pulled the duvet up to his chin, then reached out to the lamp on the bedside table and switched it off.

The room was in darkness.

Angel immediately whisked back the duvet, sat back up on the edge of the bed and put the slippers and the dressing gown back on.

It was going to be a busy night.

* * *

It was just after 2 a.m. on Friday, 30 April when, working in the dark, Angel finished removing the bulbs from the bedside lamp and the light suspended from the ceiling so that the bedroom would only be illuminated by the light on the landing when the door was opened. The rest of his preparations he had managed with the aid of the tiny lightbulb in the battery clock and a screwdriver he'd contrived from the nail file.

He put the post he had separated from the oak bed, with its top knob of hard wood, in position behind the door. Then, with aid of the light in the clock, he found his way back to the telephone on the bedside table and lifted it out of its cradle.

His call was answered by the tired voice of Hans. 'Yes, Angel? *Have you seen the time*? What do you want?'

'I can't sleep with all this on my mind. If I told you where the diary is, do you think I could go home . . . sleep in my own bed?'

Hans leapt in. 'Of course.'

Angel smiled, replaced the handset, gave the phone cable a mighty tug until it broke away from its connection and then tossed it onto the bed.

Then he took up his position behind the door. He listened intently, biting his lip as he waited for Hans to arrive.

He heard a key enter the lock.

Hans called out. 'Stand back, Angel. Stand well back. Remember I've got a gun.'

Angel rushed silently to the far side of the room. 'Don't worry, I remember.'

Angel had earlier detached a door with a large mirror fastened to it from one of the wardrobes and placed it in an upright position against the wall directly opposite the bedroom door. It was sited carefully so that anybody standing in the doorway to the bedroom would immediately see a reflection of themselves, partly in silhouette. In the atmosphere of wariness and distrust, the incomer would see the figure as an enemy, particularly if the reflection happened to be wielding a gun.

Angel only needed Hans to be confused for two seconds.

He then resumed his position behind the door.

The key turned and the door opened a crack.

Angel gripped the bedpost.

Hans pushed the door all the way back.

'Put the light on, Angel,' he said.

As Hans felt along the wall for the switch, his eye caught his own reflection in the mirror. 'Oh! Put that gun—'

But he never finished the sentence. The bed post splintered across Hans's cranium and sent him tottering to the floor.

Angel then grabbed his gun, checked that the key was in the lock, rushed out onto the landing, closed the bedroom door, turned the key two revolutions and withdrew it from the lock.

As he was quietly congratulating himself, another door on the landing opened and Jack the driver came out in his pyjamas and dressing gown. He was carrying a small pile of laundered clothes.

Angel turned and pointed the gun at him.

Jack froze in the open doorway. He stared at the gun and his eyes opened wide, showing shining black pupils in an ocean of white. He dropped the clothes and put up his hands.

'I'm not like the others, you know, Mr Angel,' he said. 'I just look after them. I was engaged as Mr Velleman's valet and chauffeur. I don't do anything bent or dishonest, you know.'

Angel pulled a severe face and said, 'Any help you give to the police will be taken into consideration when you are sentenced, I will see to that.'

Jack looked down at the clothes on the landing carpet.

'These are *your* clothes, sir,' he said. 'All clean and pressed.'

'Leave them,' Angel said. Then, pointing at the room behind the valet, he added, 'Is there anybody through there?'

'My wife, sir, Clara. She is the housekeeper here. She's fast asleep. I don't want to disturb her. If she's woken up, she can be very . . . dangerous . . . difficult.'

Angel thought he could believe the little man, but he needed to be certain.

'Wake her up. Bring her out here. But try any tricks and you'll pay for it — and that goes for your wife too. Understand?'

Jack nodded and rushed off.

Angel put the gun on a chest of drawers on the landing, and gathered up his laundered clothes from the floor. He removed his pyjamas, put on his trousers and pulled up the zip.

Angel heard a woman's voice getting louder. ' . . . I don't believe it. Have you seen the time?'

Jack said, 'Don't be difficult, Clara. I can't help it. He's a copper. And he's got a gun. We got to do what he says.'

'I think it's time we got other jobs,' the woman said. 'I never did like it here . . . no friends allowed . . . all men and all crooks . . .'

Angel quickly snatched up the gun from the chest of drawers as he stepped into his shoes.

Jack came through the doorway onto the landing. He was followed by a slim, willowy woman in her thirties. She was about twenty-five centimetres taller than her husband — and even taller than Angel himself, he reckoned. She was dressed in a fluffy dressing gown, had a mass of dishevelled fair hair, smooth skin, half closed eyes and a permanent pout.

When she saw the gun Angel was holding, it commandeered all her attention and she stopped talking.

Angel looked at her. 'You're the housekeeper here?'

'Yes, sir. Me and Jack are looking for other jobs. We didn't know we were getting mixed up with a bunch of crooks.'

'You know where everybody sleeps?'

'I make the beds, sir,' she said with a smile. 'Of course.'

Angel noticed how pretty and small her mouth was. 'Wait just there then, Mrs, er . . .'

'Clara, sir,' she said. 'Just Clara.'

Angel nodded then turned to Jack. 'Come over here by the door.'

He pointed to the door of the room that had been nominated as his bedroom for the night. Then he banged on the door with butt of the gun. 'Hans, stand back from the door.'

Angel unlocked the door and opened it halfway, but held on to the knob. Immediately over the top of it came a section of the bed leg. It hit Angel on the neck but it had no force behind it. It dropped on the floor and he kicked it out of the way.

'I warn you, Hans,' Angel said, 'If I see any part of you, I'll put a bullet through it.'

Then he turned to Jack and waved him inside the bedroom with the gun.

Jack couldn't get away from it fast enough. He backed into the room, his eyes fixed constantly on the gun until he was on the other side of the door.

Angel closed it, locked it and took out the key.

Still holding the gun and standing well away from the housekeeper, he finished getting dressed. He put an arm into his shirt. 'Tell me, who else is staying in the house tonight, Clara?'

She smiled and fluttered her thick eyelashes. 'There's Mr Velleman, Mr Starr and Dr Hart, sir.'

'Anybody else?'

'No . . . well, there are the two guards in the security station at the front gate, sir.'

'They don't come into the house?'

'No, sir. Well, I've never seen them in the house.'

Angel thought they might be from an agency and not part of the gang.

He put on his suit coat and checked the pockets, relieved to find that his phone and miniature recorder were still there. He didn't check to see whether they had been interfered with or not.

'Right,' he said, looking across at Clara. 'Show me the rooms where Velleman, Starr and Hart sleep.'

She pointed towards the stairs. 'They are all down one, sir. To the second floor. And they're apartments.'

'I'll follow you,' Angel said. 'Be *very* quiet.'

Clara pointed out the three doors, whispering each occupier's name in turn.

Angel nodded and smiled.

Suddenly Clara's eyes flashed like she had heard something.

Angel felt a jolt of panic. There was nowhere to hide.

Clara backed herself into a dark corner of the old corridor and pulled Angel close to her. He felt the warmth of her stomach and thighs against his. He looked down and there was just enough light to see her dressing gown was undone and the full length of one leg from her ankle to her waist was exposed. She gave him a sweet smile of artificial embarrassment.

It was just at that point that she lifted a hand up to the back of her neck. In a split second, Angel instinctively reached up to the slim wrist of that hand. He squeezed it and twisted it sharply.

She gasped with pain.

He pulled away from her as the slimmest, sharpest stiletto fell harmlessly from her hand onto the carpeted landing floor.

Angel stuck the gun hard into her back and whispered, 'Do you think I was born yesterday, sweetheart? That I won't pull the trigger on this gun if you try another cheap trick like that?'

He looked around for somewhere to dispose of the stiletto and kicked it under a large chest of drawers on the corridor.

'You are not human,' she said. 'You're as hard as nails.'

'Fasten your dressing gown and make your way upstairs. I'll be right behind you.'

He locked Clara in the room with her husband and Hans, and crept back downstairs to Hart's room. It was the door nearest the stairs. He tried the handle. It was unlocked. He slipped quickly into the room and closed the door behind him.

He was in darkness. He stood where he was with his back pressed against the wall. He waited there a few seconds.

A small amount of light came in through the window and from the landing under the door. It showed some of the furniture in silhouette.

He could make out a bookcase, a television and a doorway. He made for the doorway and bumped into an easy chair. He edged around it and reached the door, which he found to be ajar. He pushed it slightly and it squeaked.

It needed oil.

Angel cringed. He stopped moving, stopped breathing. He waited for some reaction. There was none.

He pushed the door a little further.

It squeaked again. He stopped.

A man's voice from the dark inside the room said, 'Who's there?'

Angel took in a mouthful of air. He hesitated, then decided he would have to make the best of it. He pushed the noisy door fully open and stepped into the room.

He could just make out the outline of the head and shoulders of a figure in a bed, a lampshade on a bedside table and a large piece of furniture on another wall.

'Police,' Angel said as he groped for a light switch. 'I have a gun on you. Put your hands where I can see them.'

He found the switch. The light came on.

Angel blinked and screwed up his eyes as he looked across at the bed and the man in pyjamas. It was William Hart, wiping his eyes.

'Angel!' he said with a sneer.

'I don't like you either, Hart,' Angel said. 'You are one of the most twisted men I know, so don't make a false move. I could earn a medal for killing you, so don't tempt me. Get out of bed, and put on your slippers and dressing gown. Slowly.'

Hart whipped back the duvet, and swivelled round so that he could tuck his feet into his slippers on the carpet.

Suddenly Angel heard heavy breathing from behind.

He glanced back. It was Oscar Starr. He was standing in the sitting-room doorway holding a gun and pointing it directly at him. Angel looked down at it.

In that second, Hart lifted the pillow from the bed and picked up a gun he had concealed there. He too aimed it straight at Angel.

Angel looked from one gun to the other and sighed. His heart bounced down to his stomach and back.

'Drop it, Angel,' Starr said.

It looked to Angel like the end of the line . . .

'Don't kill him yet, boys,' said the heavy voice of Alexander Velleman.

His huge form, clad in pyjamas and dressing gown, appeared just behind Starr.

'We have some very important business to transact with Inspector Angel before he can leave us. For ever.'

FOURTEEN

The White House, near Sheffield
Friday, 30 April, early morning

Meanwhile, outside in the early-morning air . . .

A helicopter hovered noisily over one of the major south-westerly routes in and out of Sheffield. The very loud, raucous and regular noise of the mighty engine powering the blades cut through the early-morning mist.

Next to the pilot was DI Harris. He had a map on his knee. Behind them were four special assault policemen, each in protective gear and armed with Heckler and Koch sub-machine guns.

Harris ran his hand impatiently through his hair. 'No. This is *not* the road. It must be the next one parallel to it.'

'Roger,' said the pilot. The sound of the noisy engine increased, and the helicopter banked and travelled east for a second. Then the engine quietened a little.

'Is this the road?' the pilot said.

'Should be. We want Whitehouse Road. From Whitehouse Road, it's a short private drive to a large white house set in three acres. Can't you drop any further?'

'Only if I want to lose my licence.'

Harris shook his head.

The pilot said, 'Is *this* Whitehouse Road?'

'I can't see a sign anywhere.' Harris looked down at the map on his lap. 'I need a road sign or a landmark.'

'There's a church over there,' the pilot said.

Suddenly Harris became excited. '*There it is!*' he called. 'Big white house in huge grounds.'

The pilot said, 'I see it.'

Harris turned round and shouted above the noise of the engine, to the officers patiently waiting in the tail, 'We've found it.' Then he pointed downward and said, 'We're going down. Have a closer look.'

The helicopter engine drowned his words, but they read his lips.

As they reached around twenty metres above the tallest tree in the grounds, Harris turned to the pilot. 'Impressive, isn't it?'

'Is that an antique Rolls-Royce at the front door?' the pilot said.

'Yes. That'll definitely be the place. That old Rolls is the pride and joy of Alexander Velleman, the villain we are after.'

The pilot nodded. 'And there's half a dozen other cars round the side of the house. If he needed a change.'

* * *

Angel was searched by Hart and Starr on the spot. They found the key in his pocket.

Velleman's lips tightened. He wrinkled his nose. 'That's the key to the guest room.' He turned to Starr. 'Oscar, go up and see what's happened there. Jack's not answering the bell. Neither is Clara.' Then he turned to Hart. 'And where is Hans? Go and find him. There is something wrong. And report to me in the "theatre". I'm taking Angel down there. I have been patient long enough.'

At the mention of the word theatre, Hart and Starr exchanged knowing glances, and Hart smirked grimly before they both rushed off.

Angel saw the reaction and it set him thinking.

'Come on, Angel,' Velleman said, waving the gun at him. 'Keep heading down until you run out of stairs.'

Velleman directed him down to a small room in the basement. It was powerfully illuminated with stark white strip lighting. When he switched on the lights, the filaments blinked several times until they settled into a constant glare.

Angel could see that almost everything was white. The walls were mostly covered with mirrors. A white chair stood in the centre of the room, and over it was a large round light that could be raised, lowered or tilted as needed. There were several chairs around the periphery, a white telephone on the wall and a white porcelain sink in the corner.

When Angel saw the set-up, he became disturbed. He had heard what Brian Fellowes had suffered at Velleman's hands and what Gloria Van Haven had endured at Robertson's. Were they about to do something similar to him?

He gritted his teeth as he thought about it.

But there was one big difference. At the time they were murdered, both Fellowes and Gloria had outlived their usefulness. But in this case, Angel knew where Gloria's book was. Nobody else did. And until Velleman had possession of it, Angel still had something left to bargain with. Of course, that wouldn't stop them from breaking an arm or two, inflicting pain on him in the meantime. He must hold out against them. He must tell them nothing about the book. And he must let no opportunity to escape pass him by.

'The beautiful chair in the middle is for you,' Velleman said.

Angel looked at it. He didn't like what he saw.

Velleman pulled the face of a monster. 'Sit,' he said, with another wave of the gun.

Angel did as he was told.

Velleman said, 'Put your hands behind your back.'

Angel saw his hands behind the chair in a mirror reflecting back onto another mirror. There seemed to be two metal handcuffs or sleeves behind the chair, joined by a chain.

Angel reckoned that, as Velleman would probably need both hands to hold and lock each cuff, at some point he would have to put down the gun.

And he was right.

He saw it through the mirrors. When it happened, Velleman left the gun resting on the back of the chair. Angel quickly pulled up both arms and reached out for it. He misjudged its actual position and knocked it onto the floor. Velleman bent down to pick it up. But Angel was faster. He leaped out of the chair and pushed Velleman away. Caught off-guard, his huge opponent finished up in a heap on the floor in the corner.

Angel picked up the gun.

A shot rang out from the door.

It shattered a floor tile two inches from Angel's foot.

'Drop it, Angel!' a voice said. It was William Hart. He was standing in the doorway holding the smoking gun. 'Drop it, or I'll blow your effing foot off.'

Angel knew he was beaten again.

The gun thumped on to the white floor tiles.

'And put your hands up,' Hart said.

Angel's usual buoyancy and confidence deserted him. He was in a very dark place. That was probably his very last chance and he had fluffed it. He was going to have to steel himself to suffer great pain or even death.

Velleman picked up the gun and stood up. He brushed the hair out of his eyes, then turned to Angel. 'I am running out of patience with you. You'll find out it doesn't pay to cross Alexander Velleman.'

It was the sort of excessive Nero-type language Angel expected from a madman like Velleman.

Angel looked away from him. All he could think of was how to escape this trap, how to put Velleman and his gang in prison for life.

Velleman's lips pulled back in a grimace. He looked across at Hart and nodded his appreciation of his timely intervention.

'There's something else, Alex,' Hart said. 'Hans, Peter and Clara were locked in the guest room. Angel is responsible for putting them there.'

Velleman glared at Angel. 'Yes, Mr Clever Policeman, you will pay for all of this in due course.'

The white phone on the wall rang.

Velleman snatched it up angrily. 'Yes?'

'This is Fiske on the front gate. I want Mr Velleman, please.'

'Velleman speaking. What is it?' he snapped.

'Well, sir, there's been a helicopter hovering around Chipchase Avenue and Whitehouse Road for the last five minutes or so. Now it's right overhead . . . I think it's here for us. It's lining up to land on the forecourt of the house—'

Velleman's face went scarlet. '*What*? You must not let it land. It must not land on my property! See to it. Send up some warning shots.'

Angel's face brightened. His coded message to Mary about feeding the goldfish had been duly delivered, and here was the result.

Velleman replaced the phone in its holster, tightened his grip on the gun and pointed it meaningfully at Angel.

Angel suddenly thought he was going to pull the trigger . . . that his life was over. The realisation made him feel empty and hollow inside, like he was filled with ice-cold air. He stared back at Velleman.

Hart suddenly said, 'Do you want *me* to do it, Alex?'

Velleman seemed to hesitate, then he said, 'No. And if I had wanted him dead, I wouldn't need any assistance from you or anybody else.'

Then he looked across at Hart. 'There's some rope in that cupboard. Tie to the chair and come upstairs. Be quick about it. I need you up there. I need *everybody* up there.'

Then he dashed out of the room shouting, 'Change of plan! Change of plan! Everybody upstairs and outside at the front of the house.'

* * *

The pilot gasped as he accelerated out of the line of fire. 'They're shooting at us!'

A bullet whistled through the see-through plastic floor, grazed the pilot's boot and lodged in the cabin roof.

'Bloody hell!'

The helicopter rapidly gained height and banked to the right, away from the scene.

'They must be mad,' DI Harris said. He took out his mobile and tapped in a number.

'Or desperate,' the pilot said. 'If they hit the rotor or the fuel tank, it could be the end of us. I can't risk that.'

Harris said, 'What *can* we do? Angel is in there, on his own. Mary Angel said he went after Velleman by himself. I know he needs our help. Just a minute. I'm ringing HQ for reinforcements.'

He gave directions to a dispatcher for urgent backup on the ground and ended the call. 'OK, they're on their way. But it will take half an hour or more before they can get here. What can we do *now*?'

'I can land this crate almost anywhere, but not in a hail of bullets,' the pilot said.

'Can you land in the backyard? It looks big enough.'

'If there are no aerials or cables across it.'

'I don't know!'

'Can your men vacate this crate in a couple of seconds, literally? That will give me the chance to rapidly gain height and avoid their firepower.'

'I'm sure they can.'

* * *

'Get in the chair, Angel,' Hart said, waving the gun in its direction.

Angel slowly climbed back in.

When he was settled, Hart swivelled the chair round, until Angel had his back to the cupboard by the sink. Hart opened it and took out the rope.

At that moment, Oscar Starr put his small bald head round the door of the theatre. His bushy eyebrows shot up. 'Where's the boss?'

Hart looked across at him. 'Upstairs. Look, Oscar, will you hold a gun on this man while I get him tied up?'

Starr nodded, pulled out his gun and pointed it at Angel's chest.

Hart pushed his own gun into his pocket, swivelled the chair back round and then fastened Angel's wrists together at the back. Then he put a loop round his body and the chair and secured him to the chair. He pulled the knots tight then swivelled the chair so that the remaining rope went round Angel about fifteen times. Then he fastened the end of the rope to the back of the chair.

Hart looked up at the little man. 'Thanks, Oscar.'

'He'll not get out of that in a hurry. Now, must see what Alex wants.'

'I'll join you,' Hart said.

They both rushed off.

Angel watched them go. He had to agree that Hart had made an excellent job of tying him up. He wriggled and pulled, but found hardly any slack at all. He rested then spent another few minutes pulling and pushing, but it was a waste of time and energy. There were sixteen loops of rope binding him to the chair, and his arms were tied so tight at the wrists that he couldn't use his hands at all. He was well and truly locked down.

He looked round for sharp blades, glass bottles . . . anything he could smash to get a cutting edge, but there was nothing. Only the big mirrors on the walls, but he couldn't get out of the chair to break them.

He tried to rest, and closed his eyes. It was very quiet. He wondered what was happening up above, and how he was going to get out of this place.

Suddenly, cold slim fingers touched his cheek and gently moved to his mouth.

A cold shiver of fear ran down his spine. He opened his eyes.

A woman's face was smiling down at him.

It was Clara.

He sighed.

She was wearing a white summer dress with the occasional bunch of flowers printed on it.

'What do you want, Clara?'

'That's not much of a greeting, considering you're all tied up. And here I am, beautiful, free and uncommitted,' she said.

Angel thought for a second. 'Beautiful, yes. But uncommitted?'

Clara smiled. 'Uncommitted to a man, to a cause, to anything . . .'

'I thought you were married to the chauffeur.'

Her face changed. 'Huh. Well yes, if you call him a man. He's a dwarf. But he's free and easy, as I am.' She climbed onto his lap.

Angel was helpless to stop her.

He noticed her soft pink shoes, like ballet slippers on her small feet.

She wriggled on his lap and stomach until she was comfortable. Then she smiled, put one arm round his neck and with the other hand, she caressed his cheek.

'I want a man to sweep me off my feet, take me in his arms and make mad, passionate love to me for a week, relaxing only for chilled champagne and smoked salmon.'

'I thought you were a loyal member of Alexander Velleman's gang.'

'I am a loyal member of Clara Smith's gang.'

'Hmm. And what do you want from me?'

'Well, a bit of attention, for a start,' she whispered.

Then she gave him a kiss on the cheek. It was a long, gentle, moist kiss.

Angel felt a stirring in his loins. He took a long second look at her. She *was* beautiful.

'I can't give anyone much attention trussed up like a turkey for Christmas, can I? And I *am* married, you know,' Angel said.

'Isn't everybody? So what? So am I. Three times. Who's counting?'

'Are you going to get me out of this . . . mess, Clara?'

She smiled. 'Not so fast. What do I get out of it?'

Fearing the answer, Angel asked, 'What do you want?'

'I want *you*,' she said. Then she pulled up her dress to reveal a long slim stockinged leg with a stiletto in a holster tucked behind a suspender. She withdrew the blade, pulled down the dress, and made it straight and tidy.

The sight of another stiletto in her hands quickened Angel's pulse and made his mouth dry.

She giggled as she waved the razor-sharp blade in front of his nose, scrutinizing his face for a reaction.

Her eyes shone so brightly that Angel wondered if they had some sort of evil light behind them. He would have to be careful what he said and not show a morsel of fear.

He swallowed then said brightly, 'Ah. Good of you, Clara. Does that knife cut through rope easily?'

She frowned, thought about it for a moment or two and then said in a bored voice, 'I suppose so.' Then she said, 'Now you are getting subtle. I don't like crafty people. It's something that happens to men. You give them one sip and they take a yard!'

Angel didn't know what to say.

Her mood changed again.

'You want to know how sharp this stiletto is?' she said. 'Watch this.' She put the pinpoint of the blade into the lapel of Angel's jacket and dragged it downwards about six inches. It easily cut through the Reid & Taylor worsted, exposing the cream-coloured padding inside.

Clara gazed studiously at her handiwork. Then she burst out laughing.

Angel glared at the mess. He was furious but knew he must not show it. He wasn't sure how to react. The wrong response could result in his death.

Clara kept laughing.

Then he had an idea and joined in with forced laughter.

After a few moments he said, 'I bet it won't cut through these ropes as quickly! If you had any consideration for me, you would at least cut my hands free. I can't do anything as long as they are tied together.'

She turned, kneeled up on his lap and leaned over his shoulder. She saw his arms bound tightly at the wrists. She reached over the back of the chair, and with three twists of the stiletto, she severed the rope.

Angel pulled his arms free. He sighed and rolled his shoulders several times as he brought his hands out in front. 'That's better,' he said as he unravelled the loose bits of rope from his wrists 'You should have done that before.'

Clara sat back down on his lap. She still had the stiletto in her hand.

Angel now had a free arm to support Clara's back. He pulled her in, lowered his head, cuddled her close, then made a mental apology to Mary as he gave Clara a long, lingering kiss, at the same time gently massaging her back with his other hand.

When he pulled away, Clara was smiling, her eyes closed.

She opened them to gaze at him. Angel smiled back. Neither spoke for a few moments.

'Now, are you going to give me that knife to cut these?' he said, tapping the loops of rope round his middle.

She pursed her lips, smiled and shook her head. 'I don't know.' Then dreamily she added, 'One kiss doth not a summer make.'

Angel reached out to her hand, opened her fingers and took the stiletto, closing her fingers back up.

She didn't attempt to stop him.

He eased her away from him.

Her face suddenly changed. She glared at him angrily. 'What are you doing?' she said.

He grinned and she watched him begin to pull up the loops of rope with the stiletto. He cut through each with one pull, and felt relief with each cut.

He had cut several when she suddenly started trying to take the stiletto from him. 'Give me that back!'

'No. No,' Angel said and carried on cutting the ropes.

She tried again but Angel gently pushed her away and continued the cutting.

She gave up. 'That's not fair. You're stronger than me.'

Angel said, 'Physically, men usually are.'

Clara wrinkled her nose. '*Men!* Huh! It's not fair. Men have all the advantages.'

Angel checked that he had cut all the loops round his middle, and satisfied that he was completely free, he put the stiletto carefully into his inside jacket pocket. Then placing his hands under Clara's back and knees, he stood up.

The door suddenly opened.

Still holding Clara in his outstretched arms, Angel turned to face it.

'Who are you?' Angel said.

Clara took the opportunity of reaching inside Angel's jacket and taking out the stiletto. She concealed it under a fold of her sleeve, then put her arms back around his neck, content to be held by him.

Angel knew that she'd taken it, but was more concerned about who was at the door.

Two middle-aged men in dark suits came in. 'Excuse me, sir,' the older one said, 'but the security gate was unmanned and . . .'

Angel noticed that both men had their eyes locked on Clara.

The older man continued, 'The front door was open and when nobody answered the bell, we simply came in. We've been all round the ground floor looking for somebody . . . and kept shouting and knocking on doors. We heard your voices so that's why we're here. We didn't mean to intrude.'

Angel looked from one to the other. He didn't recognise either of them, but on closer inspection they did seem familiar. Could they be the same two men he had seen in the navy-blue car? The men he'd last seen parked outside the Travellers' Hotel?

'Do you have a navy-blue car with blacked-out windows?'

'Yes, sir. That's us.'

Angel didn't think they were armed. 'What can I do for you?' he said.

Clara's arms tightened around Angel's neck. 'Oh my God. I know them. I've seen them before.'

The younger man said, 'I would advise you to put that person down somewhere and leave her to us, sir. She is a dangerous individual.'

Angel said, 'Who are you?'

'Security officers from the—'

'They're screws from the prison,' Clara screamed. 'I know who you are. But I'm not going back with you.'

The older one took out an official-looking paper and unfolded it. 'We are security officers from Rane Hill Hospital for the criminally insane. This is a warrant for Clara Louise Smith, who escaped from the security hospital on the second of July last. We had a tip-off that she was living with her husband at this address. Are you her husband, sir?'

'No.'

'I am not going back with them, Michael,' Clara said. 'Don't let them sweet-talk you into letting them take me.'

'No. I'm a police officer,' Angel told the men from the hospital. 'And this woman has just helped me to regain my liberty. She deserves every consideration you can offer her. I should be assisting other police with the arrest of the gang who live here. Before I pass her over to you, I must tell you that Clara Smith has a stiletto up her left sleeve.'

Her eyes flashed angrily. 'Oh, Michael!' she snapped.

The older man came up to Clara, still in Angel's arms.

She shrank away from him.

'If you would put her down, sir . . .' he said.

Angel was still standing by the chair they had been sharing. It was the obvious place. He turned towards it.

'I'm not going back to prison, Michael,' she yelled.

'Now, now, Clara, don't be afraid,' Angel said gently. 'It's a hospital, not a prison.'

'*I'm not going back with them!*'

Angel leaned forward and placed her gently down on the chair.

She promptly reached up her sleeve for the stiletto, pulled it out and in a split second it was in her chest up to the hilt.

Angel gasped in horror at what he was seeing. 'Clara, *no*.'

Blood spurted out onto his tie.

He pulled away from the chair.

The two men from the hospital stood, motionless and open-mouthed.

Clara's heart continued to beat for several seconds but simply pumped out blood that ran down her skin and the white collar of her dress. The life was draining out of her. Her head dropped back, and she stared at the ceiling, her eyes wide open.

'May the Lord have mercy . . .' Angel whispered.

'I came up to her to take the stiletto,' the older man said. 'If only I had been quicker.'

'It was better than her sticking it into somebody else,' the younger man said.

'But what a waste of a young life.' Angel shook his head and turned away.

FIFTEEN

The White House, near Sheffield
Friday, 30 April, early morning

'Are you ready for a rapid exit?' the helicopter pilot shouted over the deafening engine noise.

DI Harris put on his helmet, fastened the chin strap, and lifted his Heckler and Koch submachine gun. He looked behind him at his squad of four specially trained men — all similarly equipped.

They put up their thumbs for him to see — the sign that they were equally ready and eager to go.

Harris nodded then stuck out his fist with the thumbs-up sign to the pilot, who nodded and bit his lip.

Harris picked up a loud hailer, put it on a strap around his neck, opened the helicopter door and fastened it back

Nobody spoke. The only sounds were the deafening grinding of the engine and the constant repetitive whirring of the propellers.

The helicopter was about two miles away from the target, hovering over a small area of grass. The pilot first gained height to avoid being an easy target for Velleman's guns, then at speed he raced to a predetermined position over the extensive back garden of the White House. There, he found a clear lawn area near the swimming pool and descended rapidly.

Before the skids hit the deck, Harris jumped onto the grass. The other men were close behind.

The helicopter began its rapid ascent to safety in seconds.

Harris said, 'Spread out and take cover.'

* * *

Angel wasn't sure he would ever recover from the experience of having Clara Smith die in his arms. The horror of watching her stick the stiletto into her chest would be a perpetual video logged into his memory.

He accepted that he probably couldn't have done anything to change the tragic course of events, but it was a vivid illustration of the ease and speed at which one could lose one's life.

As distressed as he was, he had to put it behind him.

He was still in great personal danger.

Angel made his way up the basement steps to the open door in the hallway. Halfway up he heard footsteps running across the hall to the drawing room. He held back and approached cautiously. He wasn't armed. He peered through the gap between the door and its jamb. He saw the backs of Starr, Hart, Hans and Jack Smith rushing into the drawing room — then Velleman lumbering up behind them, toting a small, bluish handgun. Angel thought it was a Beretta Tomcat. A deadly weapon.

Then suddenly, Angel saw Velleman stop in the hall, looking thoughtful.

Velleman turned round and went back towards the open front door. Angel saw him stop again. He glanced towards the study door.

He went into the study, leaving the door open.

Angel was curious. He silently crossed the hall and looked through the doorway. He saw Velleman pull a picture off the wall, revealing a small safe. He quickly tapped in the combination, opened the safe, and took out a bulky white plastic shopping bag. He reached further in and came out with a thick wodge of twenty-pound notes. He stuffed them in his pocket.

Angel took cover behind a long curtain as Velleman rushed out of the study, crossed the hall and went out through the open front door. He was still holding the white plastic bag.

Angel crossed the hall and peered round the front door jamb.

The old Rolls-Royce was parked outside on the drive. Velleman got into the driving seat. The engine purred into life and the limousine glided quickly away.

Angel watched the old car whizz through the unmanned security gate and ran his hand through his hair in exasperation. He rubbed his chin. His own car should be somewhere around, he thought. He dashed down the steps onto the drive, heading for the right-hand side of the house — but the route was blocked with outbuildings and a path that led only to a gymnasium. He turned back and tried the other side and was rewarded with the sight of four cars, including a beautiful silver-grey Bentley as well as his own more modest BMW, spotlessly clean, polished and parked neatly side by side.

He dashed towards the BMW, hoping it wasn't locked and the keys were in the ignition. It wasn't, and they were. He had a brief moment of elation. He started the engine, let in the clutch and was through that unmanned security gate like an unfed greyhound chasing an electric hare.

Although he drove as fast as he could, he didn't seriously expect to catch up with Velleman. But he was determined to try rather than standby and let the monster escape.

When Angel reached the main road, he had to decide which way to turn. He reckoned that Velleman would surely turn left and make for Porley . . . probably the Traveller's Hotel. He would still hope to get possession of Gloria's journal. If Velleman *had* turned right, it would suggest that he was stupidly making a run for it, presumably to a place where he could hide from the law for the rest of his life.

Angel credited him with more intelligence than that.

He turned left to Porley and put his foot down.

* * *

Starr, Hart, Hans and Jack arrived in the drawing room and promptly took up defensive positions. Hans and Hart pulled out a heavy old oak table, put it on its side and stationed themselves behind it. Starr took up a position behind an upholstered chair, and Jack behind a big settee.

They all looked anxiously out of the French windows to the swimming pool and beyond.

'Where's Alex?' Starr said.

Jack said, 'I'll find him.'

The little man went back into the hall. He saw the front door was still open. He ran across the hall to it and looked outside. When he saw that the Rolls had gone, his eyebrows shot up and his mouth dropped open. He rushed back to the drawing room.

'The boss's gone!' he said. 'He's taken the Roller.'

Starr said, 'The bastard!'

'What are we going to do?' Hans said.

'We fight them and win,' Hart said. 'There can't be many of them. It's such a little chopper. There can't be more than four or five.'

'They've nothing on me . . . unless they get that diary,' Starr said. 'They can't prove a thing against me.'

Hart's jaw tightened. 'Aren't you lucky?' he said. 'If they get their hands on me, I'll be back inside for twenty years and some.'

Starr nodded, then looked across at the large, fair-haired man. 'How do you stand, Hans?'

'Same as you, Mr Starr. They've no evidence against me — unless they find that damned diary.'

Jack said, 'And I'm here as a chauffeur and valet. They've nothing on me at all.' He didn't sound convinced though.

Suddenly they heard a commanding voice through a loud hailer. It was DI Harris. He was speaking from behind the shower cubicles in the backyard.

'Now hear this. This is the police. We have reason to believe that armed criminals operate from these premises. The house is surrounded. Throw out your weapons, and come out with your hands up. You have sixty seconds. If you are innocent of any crime, you have nothing to fear.'

Hans's face was red. His breath coming fast. 'What are we going to do, Mr Starr?'

Hart said, 'They're bluffing. There's a handful of them out there, if that.'

Starr frowned. 'If you throw out your gun,' he said, 'you obviously demonstrate that you are in possession of a gun. Possession with intent is a mandatory five-year sentence in—'

Before Starr could say any more, Hart squeezed the trigger of his gun, causing a deafening sound and shattering the glass in one of the French windows.

Starr, Hans and Jack turned to look at him.

Hart was smiling. But not with his eyes. His eyes were dancing with unrestrained excitement.

Hans's fair skin went deadly pale.

Jack tugged nervously at his shirt collar.

Starr's jaw tightened. He glared angrily at Hart. 'You fool.'

'I saw a man's head bob up behind the changing cubicles,' Hart said. 'Come on. We can't surrender. They've got you for a minimum of five years. They'll have me for life. Let's get on with it. Let's give 'em hell.'

* * *

Angel was pleased to be behind the wheel of his car again. It gave him a feeling of confidence and success, although there wouldn't be much success to claim if he didn't catch Velleman and bring him to book for his heinous crimes.

* * *

Meanwhile Velleman was concentrating on the road while sucking on one of his favourite cigars. The old Rolls-Royce was making very good time on its way towards Porley along the B-road. He was on the fringe of the Pennines and the area was mountainous and rocky in places. The road wove in and out of a forest, which made it a little dark but also interesting. Then there was a curve in the road to accommodate a well-established oak tree.

He looked out for a pull-in on the left-hand side. Ahead he saw space for one car to park — leading into a field which had a wooden gate wide enough for a hay cart to pass through.

Velleman pulled into the space and switched off the engine.

He jumped out of the limousine, locked the door, then walked back about a hundred yards on the grass verge and crouched down behind a bush.

He took out his handkerchief and wiped the perspiration from his forehead.

He checked that he could see all approaching vehicles several seconds before they passed him.

Then he reached into his pocket and took out the handgun — his Beretta Tomcat — released the safety catch and laid it on the grass beside him.

* * *

Ratatat! Ratatatatat! Ratatatatatatat!

The police's submachine guns blasted away at the windows and rear aspect of the White House, making enough noise to wake the dead.

The men inside could only reply with single shots from their handguns, and for several minutes they had not even been able to fire at all for fear of being hit by the police's heavy shower of lead.

Hart said, 'This is impossible. I'm going to make a run for it. Anybody want to join me?'

Starr said, 'They say the house is surrounded. We'd never get outside.'

The hail of bullets eased, but single shots still came into the room every few seconds.

'They can't surround the place with only five or six men,' Hart said. 'Who is coming with me?'

He looked at Hans and Jack. Their nodding and raised eyebrows showed they were up for it.

Suddenly they heard DI Harris on the loud hailer. 'Now hear this. That was an example of our firepower. The house is surrounded. You cannot hope to escape. If you are innocent of any crime, you have nothing to fear. Throw out your weapons, and come out with your hands up. You have sixty seconds.'

Starr was biting his lip, and twisting a gold ring repeatedly round his little finger.

Hart said, 'Come on, Oscar. Fighting is better than prison, isn't it?'

Starr didn't immediately respond.

Hart gritted his teeth. 'Have we any other option?' he said.

Starr pulled a face like a man sucking a lemon. 'I s'pose not,' he said. And he quickly pushed the upholstered chair he had used for cover away.

Hart nodded, then turned to the others. 'Come on.'

They scrambled on hands and knees through the door into the hall.

Hart fired a further shot in the general direction of the police, to show the opposition that they were still alive and vital.

Then they rushed out of the room and across the hall.

Hart peered round the front door jamb. He could hear the uneven, raucous racket of the helicopter engine in the distance, but he couldn't see any police activity. So he led the way outside down the steps and round left to the cars.

There were three cars, including his own to choose from. He selected the highly polished, spotless Bentley which he knew belonged to Velleman. He saw the keys were in the ignition.

He turned to the others. 'Get in. Alexander won't want this now.'

* * *

'Sky One to Ground Unit,' the pilot said into his mouthpiece.

DI Harris switched on the transmitter mouthpiece. 'Ground Unit to Sky One, receiving you loud and clear.'

'Four men have come out of the house, got into a large silver-grey car . . . the car is heading for . . . it's passing through the security gate at the front of the house,' the pilot said.

Harris's eyebrows shot up. 'Oh? Thank you, Sky One. We will have to move fast. Will you pick us up ASAP?'

'Coming down now. Out.'

Harris quickly called his office on his mobile and had a hurried conversation with his sergeant.

'I want at least two patrol cars to put up a road block at map reference F9 by 1300 hours. And the Black Maria to back them up . . .'

The deafening racket of the helicopter landing close by, blowing up dust and leaves, drowned out the rest of what DI Harris was saying.

* * *

Angel was making good progress in the BMW on the road to Porley. It was a sunny day and the traffic was light. He thought that he could only be a few minutes behind the Rolls.

He felt on the shelf under the dashboard. He usually had a packet of mints there. They helped the miles roll by. He couldn't find them.

The road led him through the outskirts of a shady forest, where there was little light. Then as he came into sunshine, he had to steer round a curve in the road to accommodate an old oak tree. Then the road straightened out as he approached a bush.

Suddenly and unexpectedly he saw the old Rolls-Royce parked up ahead. That put him on his guard. He looked around for Velleman, but there was no sign of him.

Angel heard the sound of a gun being fired. At the same time he became aware that the steering on the BMW had become heavy.

It must be down to a puncture in the nearside front tyre.

Angel's thoughts were in overdrive. Where was Velleman? He must be somewhere nearby.

Angel carefully manoeuvred the BMW onto the grass verge on the left-hand side of the road and stopped. Warily, he got out of the car and looked around. Still no sign of Velleman. He realised he didn't have another spare tyre and the only weapon he had was his fists. He went to the rear of the car, opened the boot to look for something he could use to defend himself. He reached in for the jack handle.

From the bush behind the car, Velleman appeared, gun in hand.

'Good morning, Inspector Angel,' he said pompously.

Angel turned round. He was still holding the jack handle. It would be a useful weapon if he could keep hold of it. The first thing he noticed was Velleman's gun.

'Good morning, Velleman. I saw you filling your pockets and running out on your men.'

Velleman ignored the jibe. 'I thought someone might follow me. I never thought it would be you. How very convenient. Drop whatever you are holding, close the boot and slowly walk up to my Rolls-Royce. I said *slowly*.'

Angel put the jack handle in the car boot, lowered the lid and began to walk on the grass verge towards the limousine.

A car passed them by. Velleman put the gun in his pocket. 'Don't get any bright ideas,' he said. 'I won't mind a hole in the pocket of my second-best suit if it means I get to shoot you.'

They reached the Rolls and Angel turned around.

'Get in the driver's seat,' Velleman said. 'Close the door and fasten your seat belt.'

Then the big man got in the back of the car and pulled up a seat in the centre so that he was obliquely to the left of and behind his prisoner.

'Familiarise yourself with the controls,' he said, 'then drive off, *very carefully*.'

* * *

The pilot looked at DI Harris. 'That's the car down there. That Bentley. That big silver-grey job.'

Harris nodded and smiled. 'Great. Don't lose it. I expect it'll be making for Porley.' Then he took out his mobile phone. 'I'm going to check up on that road block.'

Harris spent a few minutes on the phone talking with his sergeant. Then he closed the phone and turned to the helicopter pilot, pointing to a spot on the map. 'The patrol cars will be in position there at F9, out in the country on a straight piece of road. The villains aren't far away.'

The pilot said, 'I can see a patrol car. I think it's a patrol car.'

Harris nodded. 'Yes and there's another. And a Black Maria.' His heart beat faster as he anticipated what was ahead.

'Where's the villains' car?' Harris said.

The pilot hesitated. He looked down through the transparent floor. He pressed the accelerator, put a slight turn on the blades and the helicopter climbed a couple of hundred feet at the same time banking south-west. After a few moments he said, 'The Bentley's over there.'

Harris also looked down. He spotted it and smiled.

'That's fine,' Harris said. 'Now, when I give you the nod, will you descend very quickly? Ideally, we need to be on the deck about ten metres behind the Bentley a few seconds before they reach the road block.'

The pilot grinned. 'I'll try.'

Harris then turned to the squad of men squashed in the cramped compartment behind him and briefed them. Because of the engine noise it wasn't easy. But their smiles and nods showed Harris they understood and were ready for anything.

DI Harris put on his anti-flak helmet, fastened the chin strap, and picked up his Heckler and Koch.

He looked down at the scene. The two police patrol cars and the Black Maria were in position across the road. He saw the Bentley racing down the road towards them.

Harris looked at the pilot. 'Take us down now, as *fast as you can.*'

'Here we go,' the pilot said.

The Bentley turned the corner and reached the road block with a loud screech of brakes and stopped. The limousine didn't move for a few seconds.

Meanwhile the helicopter landed just behind the limousine, and Harris and the four special assault police had leaped out and were on the road ready for action.

The Bentley began to reverse in hard lock but had to stop, slewed across the road, because the helicopter had landed in its path.

Harris and his squad let off a volley of bullets over the roof of the Bentley. Then Harris said into his loud hailer, 'You are surrounded. Throw down your guns and get out of the car with your hands up.'

From the driver's seat of the Bentley, Dr Hart pulled out a gun and fired a bullet at Harris. It hit him in the chest. He fell forward onto the road.

One of the four special assault police rushed over to him.

The other three pointed their submachine guns at Hart. Their faces showed their anger and determination.

Hart froze. His eyes bulged. He couldn't blink.

The corporal from the squad of four called out to him, 'Drop that gun or you are dead.'

Hart didn't drop it.

The policemen's faces hardened. They tightened their grip on their submachine guns.

Hart held his breath.

The gun rattled as it hit the road.

The corporal said, 'Everybody else in the car, throw out your weapons.' There was more rattling of guns on the road. There were four handguns altogether.

One of the squad collected them and took them round to the driver of the nearest one of the two patrol cars forming part of the road block. He put them in the boot of his car.

The bullet fired at Harris had been prevented from entering his chest by his protective chest armour. However the hit had winded him. The DI was now up on his feet. He quickly took back possession of his submachine gun from the squad member and checked the safety catch.

Then he said, 'Thank you, Corporal. Please carry on.'

The Corporal nodded and turned back to the Bentley. 'Now, get out of the car.'

Nobody moved for about ten seconds, then a rear door opened and Jack Smith got out.

'I shouldn't be treated like this, friends,' Jack said. 'I haven't done anything wrong . . . I just work for them. I don't know what they do.'

The corporal said, 'Tell it to the judge. Turn round. Face the car and spread your legs.'

Another squad member patted him down and found nothing.

Shortly afterward, Hans came out through the open Bentley door. He obediently put his arms on the roof of the limousine and spread his legs.

A few minutes later, the helicopter left for base, and the Black Maria was transporting the four villains in handcuffs back to the station, escorted by two police patrol cars.

'But where is Angel?' asked DI Harris.

* * *

As Angel looked down the long bonnet of the vintage Rolls-Royce he saw a road sign that read, *Porley, 2 miles.*

Velleman behind him may also have seen it, because he suddenly said, 'Stop the car. Pull over to the side.'

Angel did as he was told. Velleman was the one holding the gun.

'I have a proposition for you.'

'I don't do deals,' Angel said.

Velleman's face hardened. 'Listen carefully, Angel. This might just save your life.'

Angel shook his head slowly.

'In view of the fact that I hold all the cards,' the big man said, 'how much do you want for Gloria Van Haven's diary? I have the means to raise two hundred and fifty thousand pounds in cash, which is *more* than enough. What do you say?'

The big man then reached into his inside pocket, took out a brown cigar case, selected a cigar, and with a small cutter neatly trimmed the end.

Angel hunched his shoulders, pulled a face like he'd caught the scent of a sewer. 'That diary gives the details of a plan, conceived by you, to disgrace me by murdering an innocent man, faking evidence that could convict me of his murder, and creating a situation that makes it impossible for me to prove my innocence with any alibi. If I was to be tried, I would almost certainly be found guilty and I would be sentenced to life in prison. More importantly, it would bring disgrace on my wife, my family past and present, my friends, the force in general and Bromersley Police in particular. Conversely, presenting that diary to the Crown Prosecution Service would absolve me of any crime completely. So, Mr Velleman, there isn't enough money printed that I would accept for surrendering that diary.'

Velleman sniffed. 'Yes. Yes. I thought you might come up with that goody-goody stock Robin Hood-type reply. It worried me somewhat, until I realised that if the diary was never found and you didn't exist, I would avoid totally any sort of confrontation with the law.' He grinned icily and waved the unlit cigar around.

Angel knew that that was a possibility but he wasn't about to admit it.

'There is absolutely no risk that the diary will *not* be found,' Angel said.

Velleman pursed his lips. He rubbed his chin thoughtfully. Eventually, he put the cigar between his lips and pointed to a carved ivory knob on the dashboard. 'Push that button in, will you? It's a cigar lighter.'

Angel did as he was told. Velleman was still the one holding the gun.

'Where would the evidence against me come from?' Velleman persisted. 'Dead men don't talk.'

'You don't think that I would be stupid enough to hide the diary in a place where it would never be found, do you?'

Using the cigar as a pointer, he said, 'I'd say you hid it under a dandelion, on a silver-birch tree or in a gap in some stone wall. You hadn't much choice in the matter. I'd say that maybe only the squirrels will have the chance of reading it.'

Angel was lost for words.

'Of course,' Velleman said, 'there's still my offer of a quarter of a million pounds in cash.'

'No, thanks.'

There was a click to indicate the lighter was ready.

Angel pulled out the ivory-handled cigar lighter from under the dashboard and turned to hand it to Velleman.

Suddenly, he deliberately dropped the lighter, grabbed Velleman's right hand — the hand holding the gun — with both of his, and quickly twisted the barrel up and away from him. He yanked Velleman's hand and arm over the back of the driver's seat, twisting so that the palm was facing upwards and the elbow on the top of the back of the driver's seat, then applied downward pressure to Velleman's hand and arm.

The big man screamed an expletive, dropped the gun onto the front bench seat, and rushed his free hand to try to remove Angel's painful grip.

Angel released his hold and snatched up the gun.

'You bastard!' Velleman yelled, rubbing his arm and shoulder.

Angel gave a big sigh. He felt ultra-awake. Adrenaline was pumping round his body. He bounced out of the Rolls, leaving the driver's door open. He opened the rear door, backed off a few feet, and held up the gun. 'Come on, Velleman. Out you come.'

The big man was scrambling around the floor of the limousine for the cigar and the lighter.

'Hurry up,' Angel said. 'Leave that.'

Velleman came out of the limousine slowly, still rubbing his arm and rolling his shoulder.

'Into the front,' Angel said. 'You can drive for a change.'

* * *

It was half past four that Friday afternoon when the Rolls-Royce pulled into the pound which was part of the private parking area for police vehicles at the back of Bromersley Police Station.

Angel put Velleman in a cell and took the key down to the duty sergeant.

'I want you to charge him with the murder of Brian Fellowes. Give him something to eat, one phone call, no visitors except a brief. All right?'

'Right, sir,' the sergeant said.

'Who's on duty transport?'

'Sergeant Mallin, sir.'

Angel was soon speaking to Mallin himself.

'My BMW is on the side of the road near Porley. It's got a puncture, thanks to a certain gangster.'

'We'll sort it. We should be able to bring it in, sort out the tyres, and have it delivered to your house in no time,' Mallin said.

'That's great,' Angel said. 'Have you an unmarked car I could use until then?'

'There's one just had a service. I'll bring it round the front.'

'Thank you, Norman.'

Angel then rang DI Harris on his mobile. They were both highly jubilant. They exchanged their news and arranged to have Velleman taken to appear in Crown Court at an early date with the rest of the gang. Angel told Harris about the tragic suicide of Clara Smith, which had to be reported. He also told him that he expected to pick up the diary in the next hour or so. Harris rang off.

Angel got in the car and sped off to the wood near Porley. He parked in the Travellers' car park and climbed over the gate into the field where the burnt-out haystack still smouldered. He followed the track he had taken when he hid the diary and had no difficulty in finding it again.

Coming out of the wood he looked round. He was wary. He didn't want the book taken from him again at this late stage.

He reached the car without meeting anyone at all.

He started the car and made for home.

It was just after seven that evening when, dishevelled, tired and hungry, he put the car in his garage and then, with the diary under his coat, he made his way down the path through the back door and into the kitchen.

When Mary saw him she gasped with relief.

'Oh, Michael. Thank God you're all right. I've been so worried. You'll be hungry. Have you had a meal? What do you want? I've been sick with worry. Why didn't you phone me? What happened? What happened to last night? You look pale and drained. Let me get you something. What would you like? What's the matter with you? Why don't you answer me? Cat got your tongue?'

THE END

ALSO BY ROGER SILVERWOOD

YORKSHIRE MURDER MYSTERIES
Book 1: THE MISSING NURSE
Book 2: THE MISSING WIFE
Book 3: THE MAN IN THE PINK SUIT
Book 4: THE MORALS OF A MURDERER
Book 5: THE AUCTION MURDERS
Book 6: THE MISSING KILLER
Book 7: THE UMBRELLA MURDERS
Book 8: THE MISSING MILLIONAIRE
Book 9: THE MISSING THIEF
Book 10: FIND THE LADY
Book 11: THE MISSING MODEL
Book 12: MURDER IN BARE FEET
Book 13: THE MISSING HUSBAND
Book 14: THE CUCKOO CLOCK MURDERS
Book 15: SHRINE TO MURDER
Book 16: THE SNUFFBOX MURDERS
Book 17: THE DOG COLLAR MURDERS
Book 18: THE CHESHIRE CAT MURDERS
Book 19: THE DIAMOND ROSARY MURDERS
Book 20: THIRTEEN STEPS TO MURDER
Book 21: THE FRUIT GUM MURDERS
Book 22: THE MONEY TREE MURDERS
Book 23: ANGEL AND THE ACTRESS
Book 24: THE MURDER LIST
Book 25: THE LIPSTICK MURDERS
Book 26: THE MUSIC BOX MURDERS
Book 27: MURDER ON TIME
Book 28: ANGEL'S FINAL PROBLEM?

STANDALONE
THE GUILTY DAUGHTER

Thank you for reading this book.

If you enjoyed it please leave feedback on Amazon or Goodreads, and if there is anything we missed or you have a question about, then please get in touch. We appreciate you choosing our book.

Founded in 2014 in Shoreditch, London, we at Joffe Books pride ourselves on our history of innovative publishing. We were thrilled to be shortlisted for Independent Publisher of the Year at the British Book Awards.

www.joffebooks.com

We're very grateful to eagle-eyed readers who take the time to contact us. Please send any errors you find to corrections@joffebooks.com. We'll get them fixed ASAP.

Printed in Great Britain
by Amazon

73072414R00121